THE JESTER

THE JESTER KING FANTASY SERIES:
BOOK 2

K. C. Herbel

Epic Books Press

RICHMOND, VIRGINIA

Previous editions of this book were published under the title: "With a Jester of Kindness"

Epic Books Press
P.O. Box 358
Quinton, Virginia 23141
www.EpicBooksPress.com

Publisher's Note: This is a work of fiction. Names, characters, places, and incidents are a
product of the author's imagination. Locales and public names are sometimes used for
atmospheric purposes. Any resemblance to actual people, living or dead, or to businesses,
companies, events, institutions, or locales is completely coincidental.

Cover Artist: SelfPubBookCovers.com/Ravenborn

Ordering Information:
Quantity sales. Special discounts are available on quantity purchases by corporations, as-
sociations, and others. For details, contact the "Special Sales Department" at the address
above.

Library of Congress Control Number: 2017905242

The Jester / K. C. Herbel. -- 1st ed.
ISBN 978-1-944314-08-8

In memory of my father, whom I still miss very much. To his father, the storyteller; to my mom, for always being there, and to my wife, my best friend in this world.

GWYTHIA

CAITHNESS
SHIRE

ERIN

ALBION

DUMNONIA

LYONESSE

Book Two

THE JESTER

"Some rise by sin, and some by virtue fall."

—WILLIAM SHAKESPEARE

CHAPTER SEVENTEEN

A Change in Fortunes

As in Hillshire, Billy found that his audience at the wedding feast was reluctant to let him stop singing. Each time that he made motions to leave the stage they would protest and insist that he give them one more song. Billy felt embarrassed when he saw the other musicians standing idly nearby, so he signaled for them to come join him. They looked at each other, unsure if Billy was talking to them.

Finally Billy called, "Musicians! Come help me!"

After a moment's hesitation, the musicians gathered their instruments and went to the front of the dais where they joined Billy.

"Now we can really play some lively tunes!" he told them.

The musicians replied by smiling and adding the sounds of their instruments to his. The added musicians infused the crowd with vigor. All present were caught in the music's irresistible spell. They wished they could dance and sing forever.

In the midst of the revel, Billy spied a messenger weaving his way through the crowd. He recognized the red and gold as a member of Earl Finney's household. Billy took a quick look at the earl, who sat atop his table, singing and drinking with a great toothy grin, his arms gesturing wildly about him. *What a grand sight he is.*

The messenger pushed his way past the dancers, to the dais. He stopped momentarily to speak with the guard, who nodded and let him pass. The boy, red-faced from exertion, quickly crossed behind the table and bowed beside Lady Myrredith and Sir Hugh. The Lady of Cyndyn Hall leaned forward to hear the earl's servant over the ruckus. *I hope it's good news. Maybe Aonghas is coming!*

Lady Myrredith straightened slowly. Her face had lost its rosy color and smile. It was a hollow, pale mask.

Billy stopped playing, and the other musicians followed. Then the dancers stopped. They whined and hollered for the music to continue.

"What is it, William?" the king asked. He seemed unaware of the messenger by Myrredith's side. "Well ...? Speak up. Why have you stopped?"

Lady Myrredith rose stiffly and remained still for a moment. The king saw her face, and his face took on a solemn expression.

"Myrredith, has something happened?"

"I apologize, Majesty, I did not mean to disturb this joyous occasion."

"What is it, child?"

"I-My ..." Lady Myrredith braced herself on the table.

Billy could see Lady Myrredith's shoulders shake as she tried to control her tears. Kathryn and Gaelyn silently approached the table.

Sir Hugh stood and placed his hand on Myrredith's. "Sir Aonghas ... has died."

A rumble stormed through the crowd like far-off thunder. The hubbub was too garbled for Billy to comprehend.

Finally, the noise lessened as the king rose to his feet. "Quiet!" he shouted hoarsely. He wheezed and then fell into the throes of a violent coughing fit. After he had recovered, he turned to face down the table. "Lady Myrredith, this is news that saddens my old heart. You have our complete sympathies." Then the king fell silent for a moment as if remembering some long-forgotten time.

Lady Myrredith bowed. "Thank you, Your Majesty."

"I am sure," the king said in a commanding voice, "that no one here would wish to continue celebrating after hearing of your loss—of indeed—this loss to us all."

"Here, here!" came the response from several men in the crowd.

"No!" Lady Myrredith reclaimed some of her usual strength. "This should be a day of great gladness for the entire kingdom. I could not bear for it to be otherwise."

"But Myrredith—"

"No, Kathryn. This is your day, Highness. It means a great deal to me – to all our people."

A tremor in her voice signaled that she was cracking under the strain. However, as Eadwig put it, "she is a Cyndyn," which meant she would not allow herself to become a pitiful spectacle, nor would she budge until her will prevailed.

Princess Kathryn bowed deeply to the Lady of Cyndyn Hall. "As you wish, dear friend."

"Thank you, Your Highness." Lady Myrredith turned to King William. "I hope you will excuse me, Your Majesty, I have some packing to do."

"Of course, child."

The ward was silent as Sir Hugh escorted Lady Myrredith from the dais. Her footing faltered on the steps down, but Hugh steadied her. Those they passed bowed deeply before the dignified lady.

It was a long while before anyone felt much enthusiasm for celebrating. The musicians, being the professionals they were, tried to lighten up the atmosphere by playing cheerful festival music. Billy tried to strum along with them, but his heart just wasn't in it.

Billy wanted to go to his patron, to comfort her and cheer her up, but realized the futility in it. Instead, he decided to leave the crowd to wander through the donjon alone and sort things out.

Billy went to take his leave from King William. "Your Majesty," he said with a bow, "if I may, I would like to—"

"Retire?"

"Yes, Your Majesty."

"Of course, William. But before you go, allow me to thank you for the marvelous entertainment."

"Thank you, Your Majesty."

"I know Sir Aonghas' death must be upsetting to you," Kathryn said, "but never forget that today you made your king and myself *very* happy."

Billy bowed. "Yes. Thank you, Princess Kathryn."

The princess continued. "I guess what we're trying to say, William, is that you are welcome here anytime you wish."

"And even though ya have come with Lady Myrredith," Prince Gaelyn added, "there's no reason why ya have to leave with her."

"What?"

The prince smiled. "We'd be very glad to have ya stay."

"You can stay here with us for a while," his bride said. "The coronation is only a few days away."

The king leaned forward. "And we have been without an official court entertainer for quite some time."

Billy's mind was adrift in a sea of conflicting thoughts: *They invited me to stay ... Sir Aonghas is dead ... They need a court entertainer ... Lady Myrredith's leaving ...* He didn't know what to make of what he was hearing. He was hesitant to say anything.

"Think on it well, William," the king said.

Billy turned to leave, then turned back and bowed to the royal family. Suddenly the meaning of their invitation was clear. "I will, Your Majesty!"

* * *

Billy meandered through the halls of Orgulous for the remainder of the day. Late afternoon, he started for Lady Myrredith, only to change his mind at the last moment. He left his new lute by the door instead.

It felt as if a lifetime of experiences had been packed into one day. He couldn't focus on any one thing. There were simply too many things to consider: first his new clothes and losing his mother's ring, then missing the wedding and finding the ring, then his run-ins with Ergyfel and the king, and then the feast and Malcolm, and the prince, and Sir Aonghas and Lady Myrredith, and finally the king asking him to stay. It was dizzying. Above all else, the thing that stuck in his head was Sir Aonghas' death. It made the least sense of anything. Billy wondered if Aonghas knew how much his wife truly loved him.

Billy roamed the donjon and ended up exactly where he started. At that moment, he decided to find Sir Hugh. A passing servant informed him that he had seen the King's Champion, "headed toward the stables."

Billy thanked the man and ran from the donjon towards the kitchen and barracks. There was still a great commotion in the inner ward. Lady Myrredith had said the entertainment would carry on late into the night.

When Billy got to the inner gate, he carefully eyed the heavily shadowed outlet. He stood his ground, listening and watching for any hint of monsters.

A guard observed his trepidation. "What's the matter, boy?"

"I'm afraid of those troghouls."

The guards laughed, then one of them said, "Go on, boy. They're all gone now."

Billy peered into the dark. "Where'd they go?"

"What does it matter?" the third guard said.

"The magister took them away," the first added.

Billy nodded, then strolled into the gateway. About three steps in, he felt eyes staring at him from the shadows. His heart beat faster, and then he sprinted the rest of the way across the gap to sunlight. Behind him, the guards burst out laughing.

Billy ran to the stables to find his friend. "Sir Hugh! Sir Hugh!"

Hugh answered from inside. "Over here."

Billy walked to the stable closest to the inter-bailey wall. There was a small silver shield with a blue stripe hanging over the entrance, which told him he was in the right place.

Hugh appeared behind the gate. "Welcome, Billy."

"Hello, Sir Hugh."

"What brings you out here?"

"I was lookin' for you. Goin' for a ride?"

"No, I just prefer to take care of my mount personally, and with Splendore's temperament I think it's a necessity."

Billy laughed. He then remembered the candy he had put into his pocket and offered a piece to Splendore, who graciously accepted it.

Sir Hugh returned to grooming his horse. "What did you need? We could go riding tomorrow if you like."

"No. I mean, I'd like that, I just—there's—things really happen fast in the city."

"What do you mean?"

Billy was about to name off all the things that had happened to him that day, but decided that it was too long a list. Instead, he settled for a question. "How's Lady Myrredith?"

"I don't know." Hugh leaned over the gate. "She's a strong woman."

"She's a Cyndyn."

Hugh chuckled. "Aye, she is that! But still …"

"What?"

"She's a woman."

"A lady."

Hugh took in a deep breath and let it out slowly. His eyes studied the sky. "A very kindhearted, very faithful lady."

"He really loved her, you know?"

"What?"

"I mean …" Billy cleared his throat. "He told me so, before …"

"Aye."

The two friends became silent. Billy considered what he should do, or could do for Lady Myrredith. He looked at his companion's face. It was a map of lines portraying his concern. Billy went around the gate, into the stall, and together he and Hugh spread fresh straw on the floor.

Billy stopped and looked up. "Did ya know Sir Banarel?"

Hugh looked at his companion. "Aye, I knew him. Lady Myrredith tells me he died at your father's inn."

Billy nodded. "He was killed by a horse in our stables."

"That's what she said."

"Was he a friend of yours, Sir Hugh?"

"No."

"Wasn't he one of the king's knights?"

"The king may have knighted him, but he earned his spurs doing God-knows-what for the magister."

"So ya didn't trust him?"

"Only a fool trusts the dog sent by a wolf."

Billy decided not to pursue the question any further and returned to spreading the straw. A minute later he broke his silence.

"How long has the king been sick? I mean ... he's not that old!"

Hugh's eyebrows scrunched together. "A long time now. He fell ill just after his queen died."

"Did you hear what the king asked me?"

"When?"

"After you and Lady Myrredith left the feast."

"No."

"He and Princess Kathryn want me to stay."

Hugh dropped his armful of straw. "To stay?"

"Yes! Well, at least till after the coronation."

"What of Lady Myrredith? She will be leaving soon."

"I know." Billy frowned and pushed the straw with his foot. "I want to go with her, but I want to stay too. What should I do?"

"This is why you came to see me, isn't it?"

"Aye."

"I don't know what to tell you, Billy. You've always wanted this, haven't you—to be here, in Orgulous, with the king?"

"Aye! Who wouldn't?"

A brief smile passed over Hugh's face as he nodded. His eyes focused beyond the walls of the Royal Champion's stable.

"Me too. Since I can remember, I knew I had to be here. My mother tried to dissuade me, but I knew I had to be one of King William's knights, like my father."

"I wanted to be a knight too. All my life I played at being a knight. I practiced swordplay. I practiced my reading and writing. I was a good boy. All so that one day, if I came to Castle Orgulous, before King William, I would be worthy. But that was just a boy's dream. My friends all grew up. I did not. Eventually, I knew that I wasn't meant to be a knight, just an innkeeper."

"But not now."

"No. Thanks to you and Lady Myrredith, I think I can be more."

"Can be, or will be?"

"I don't know. My heart wants more, but my head ... I'm just simple folk—the son of an innkeeper."

"Not many people have the opportunity to follow their heart."

"Then you think I should accept?"

"I didn't say that. I was going to say that following your heart doesn't always bring you happiness."

"Why not?"

"Well, I guess it's because things are rarely the way they should be."

"Are you happy, Sir Hugh?"

"For a simple innkeeper's son, you sure have a way of asking the most confounded questions."

Sir Hugh said only a handful of words after that. He and Billy finished tending to Splendore Pomponnel and returned to the donjon. Lady Myrredith was out on the balcony when they arrived at her chambers. The room was dark, and the blue sky that had graced them all day had turned rusty behind her.

"Milady?" Hugh said quietly.

Lady Myrredith turned to face them. In the fading evening light, Billy could see that her eyes were puffy and her cheeks wet with tears. She wore a simple black dress with no jewelry, and her beautiful red hair flowed gently over her shoulders, like water in a stony brook. Billy could not help thinking how stunning she looked, even in grief.

"William, Hugh. I was beginning to think you two were lost."

"Only in thought, milady," Sir Hugh answered.

"Good," Lady Myrredith muttered. "I received a message, William ... from Kathryn. She said that you wanted to stay."

"I haven't made up my mind."

"What's to decide? This is where you should be, William! I'm sure your father wouldn't disapprove."

Billy detected a sharp, fragile edge in her tone. "It's not that." He suddenly felt homesick.

"Then what, William?"

"I don't know."

Lady Myrredith stepped towards him. "It's not me, is it? Don't worry about me, my dear, sweet William. I can take care of myself. You need to think of yourself. This is your moment! Take hold of it, and don't let go!"

She was right. She was the primary cause of Billy's hesitation. However, it was not out of pity, but friendship—the truest friendship he had ever felt. From the day he left his father, Billy's attachment to Myrredith had grown. In his heart he knew that their parting was inevitable, but he had blocked it from his mind. Now the king's offer forced him to face it. It forced him to choose between pursuing a dream and sticking by his best friend. It felt like reaching into a blazing fire to pull out a diamond.

Sir Aonghas' death and Lady Myrredith's sorrow only made deciding all the more difficult. If she didn't before, she would need him now.

Lady Myrredith walked to Billy and placed her hands on his shoulders. He looked up into her face and failed in an attempt to smile. Billy decided that this must be why Lady Myrredith had called him a terrible liar. It was always hard for him to hide the way he felt inside, especially with her.

"Don't worry, William," she said. "I won't be leaving for another day. And I shall still love you, no matter what you decide."

Billy stared at the floor between his feet. "I know."

Lady Myrredith gently lifted his chin. "I do think you should stay. You've come a long way in a very short time, but that doesn't mean you can't go further. In truth, I believe that your journey may just be starting."

Billy reached around Lady Myrredith's waist and hugged her. "I love you too, Lady Myrredith," he said, fighting back his tears. "You're the best friend I've ever had!"

Billy heard the door close and looked to find that Sir Hugh had left. Billy started to go after him but was quickly reminded by Lady Myrredith's touch that he had more important things to do than follow Hugh around. He gave his patron another squeeze and then moved to the nearest lamp and lit it. As the glow of the lamplight grew, it revealed Billy's reward from the princess resting upon a chair. The marvelous inlaid patterns of finely polished wood around the sound hole seemed to smile at him.

"Shall I play something for you, milady?"

"Yes, William. That would be wonderful."

Billy collected his lute and took a brief moment to tune it. When he looked up, Lady Myrredith was standing once again on the balcony. Her slim silhouette was surrounded by the red glow of the evening sky. Billy's heart ached, but he was determined to lift his lady's spirits. He reached into his growing repertoire and drew out a song that was light and gay, but more importantly, had made Lady Myrredith laugh. How he yearned to hear her light, birdlike laugh at that moment. It had become to him like honey to a sweet-toothed child. With that in mind, he began:

"Oh, come all ye maidens, and listen to me ..."

Billy continued on, wishing for his sweet reward. The song ended, having failed to coax the response he had desired; indeed, Lady Myrredith showed no response whatsoever. She simply stood, framed in the doorway, staring out beyond the horizon.

CHAPTER EIGHTEEN

Decisions, Decisions

B illy was roused from his sleep by a muffled thud. He sat up in bed and looked about in the darkness. The sun had not yet risen, and all was quiet. Even the birds, earliest of risers, were still. Billy concentrated until an echo of the sound that awoke him reverberated in his head. It was the sound of a door closing.

Billy jumped out of bed and threw on his clothes. He cracked his door open to look into the central chamber. The door's hinges groaned.

"Blasted noisy doors," he whispered.

He peered through the narrow opening. The room was empty. He opened the door quickly, hoping to avoid any more noisy complaints, and tiptoed across the room to the main door. He scanned the dark room before placing his ear against the door to listen. It was quiet, but then he heard the scuff of far-off footsteps. Cautiously, he opened the heavy wooden door and slipped out, being very careful not to make any sound as he brought it closed behind him.

The hall was empty except for Billy. He listened again for the footfall he had heard from behind the door and was rewarded with a distant scrape. He turned and padded down the hallway.

At several turns, Billy had to stop and listen for his prey. He didn't know whom he was following, or even why he was following. He only knew that if someone was up this early creeping around Castle Orgulous there had to be a good reason, and he wanted to know what it was.

Finally Billy came to an entryway that led into a spacious garden. He could make out a large still pool bordered by flowers, which were raised in the black cobweb shadows under several ranks of trees. He went to step through the portal but felt prickles on the back of his neck and stayed his foot.

Movement down a path on the opposite end of the pond caught Billy's attention. At that moment, he heard footsteps approaching from behind. There was nowhere to go except into the garden. Fear of being discovered forced him to descend the steps. Quietly, he slipped down a path that led into the trees. He climbed a tree until he reached a place that was well hidden but afforded a good view of the egress. Within moments, a cloaked man appeared in the archway and entered the garden. Billy held his breath as the man passed directly under him. When the man was well down the path, Billy dropped from the tree. The foreboding feeling was completely forgotten under an adrenal blanket.

A secret meeting! Maybe I'll just see who it is, and then sneak away.

Billy crept along the path just out of sight of the mysterious cloaked man. As they moved around the pond, Billy noticed that walls of the donjon enclosed the entire garden. The only way in or out was the way he had come. Billy's heart beat faster yet.

At the end of the pond, the man halted abruptly. Billy quickly slipped behind a shrub and lay down on the ground.

"My Lady!"

Billy recognized Sir Hugh's voice. *What's he sneaking around for? And with whom?*

"Hugh."

That's Lady Myrredith!

Hugh continued. "How are you?"

"Well."

Billy could not see his patron, but he could sense that she was not being entirely truthful.

"What are you doing here?" Hugh asked.

"I knew … I knew that you would be here. I was informed that you start each morning here—that is, whenever you are in Orgulous."

Billy inched closer until he could see her. She sat on a short marble bench facing the pond. Behind her stood a large, square stone, partially entwined by a hardy thorn tree.

"You are well informed," Hugh said from behind her. "Do you know why?"

"It's a beautiful spot in the morning?" Lady Myrredith rose from the bench.

"Yes, it is, but there is another reason."

Lady Myrredith paced around Hugh and placed her hand on the large square stone. "They should do something about these thorns."

"They have, but they just kept coming back stronger than before."

"The queen. Is she the reason you come here?"

"Aye. I made a vow to her."

"A vow?"

"Aye."

"But she's been dead for many years."

"And so has my father!"

Lady Myrredith studied the King's Champion. "What are you saying, Hugh? Is there some connection?"

"Mother told me that my father took a sacred oath to obey and protect the queen. I think he died keeping that oath. In fact, I think they died at the hands of the same killer."

"What?" Lady Myrredith stiffened. "Killer? I don't understand."

"Killer or killers."

"She was *murdered*?"

"Yes. Not many know."

Billy could hardly believe what he was hearing. The queen had died before his memory began, and in the many years since, he had never heard of anyone who suspected foul play in the queen's death. *How could such a thing be kept a secret?* His stomach churned.

"I heard rumors," Lady Myrredith said, "but I never... And what's your part in it?"

"I must find the man responsible, and kill him."

Billy's heart stopped. He had never heard the King's Champion speak of killing with such callousness.

"Was she really murdered?"

"On this very spot. In the middle of this great fortress! Under the nose of the royal guard!" Hugh stopped himself short of shouting. He took a deep breath and continued in a softer voice. "Mother said this was the queen's favorite sanctuary."

"Do you have any idea who did it?"

"I have my suspicions, but in this task I must be most certain. Too many years have made the trail cold. I pray to our Lord that He will some-day lead me to the caitiff, but now I'm beginning to think I'll never know."

"Perhaps the fiend has met with justice some other way," Myrredith offered. "I don't have to remind you that vengeance is the Lord's."

Hugh nodded. "Perhaps, but you didn't come here to discuss the Scriptures."

"No."

"What then?"

The Lady of Cyndyn Hall shifted her stance. "Hugh, in the light of what you just told me, what I have to say seems so trivial, but I must tell you. It's not easy for me, so please just listen." She then invited him to sit.

Hugh bowed his head to her and sat on the edge of the bench. He waited patiently while she paced in silence.

Billy's patience was almost at its end. Part of him wanted to leave, but he was afraid that in the quiet of the garden he would give himself away. He remembered the last time he had eavesdropped on his two best friends, and the burden that incident bore on his heart. Already the world felt less wondrous than the day before, being marred by the truth of the queen's death. It frightened him.

Finally, Myrredith took a deep breath and began. "Hugh, we ... I loved you. I've never known anything that could compare, but when I married Aonghas, I-I thought that you hadn't come for me because you didn't love me. Afterwards, I heard about the invasion, but it was too late. I couldn't be his wife and allow myself to feel that way about you. Please understand, I never wanted you to stay away! In fact, I-I often wished you hadn't. You were the best friend I ever had.

"When I heard that Aonghas had died, I only wanted you to hold me, to feel your arms ... Sweet Mother of Jesus, save me, that's what I wanted."

Hugh rose and took a step towards her.

Myrredith turned and placed her hands on the large square stone. "I know it's wrong, Hugh, but I need you. You deserve far more, however, all I can offer now ... is my friendship. You disappeared from my life before. I could not bear to lose you again."

Hugh knelt beside her and bowed his head. "Myrredith, my friendship, as my heart, will always be yours." Then he gingerly kissed her hand.

The first song of morning abruptly broke the silence in the garden as birds greeted the rising sun. All three visitors looked heavenward. The surrounding walls of the donjon framed the brightening sky. A lone smokelike cloud lazily wafted across the colorful empyrean tapestry, promising a splendid day of sunshine.

"You should leave now, milady."

"And you?"

"I shall linger only a moment longer. I too have many things to attend to before we depart for Hillshire."

"Then you will come with me?"

"Of course. I will not desert you again."

Myrredith reached for his hand but stopped short. "Thank you. Oh, but what about William?"

Hugh took Lady Myrredith by the elbow. "If he decides to stay, I will make arrangements with Gaelyn for his safety."

"Good. I will talk to Kathryn as well. William has won her heart, you know?"

"Aye."

"She will look after him. She promised to grant my boon."

Hugh smiled. "It means a great deal."

Myrredith nodded. "His future, perhaps mine."

"Yes." Hugh ushered Myrredith away. "Now hurry. I will meet with you later."

Hugh and Billy watched her leave, and then Hugh returned to the large dark block in front of the bench. The King's Champion knelt in front of the stone and clasped his hands together. Hugh prayed for a long while. Billy was just about to get up and sneak away when Hugh rose. It was so light now that Billy just knew he would be discovered. Fortunately, Hugh turned and left around the opposite side of the pond.

After Hugh was well out of sight, Billy sat up with a sigh. He then stood and brushed himself off.

"I'm never gonna do this again!"

Billy walked to the large stone block. He leaned over to examine its smooth face and noticed writing that had been invisible in the dim light.

The first line had only two strange words: HIC JACET. Then underneath, it read: ELEANOR, BELOVED WIFE AND QUEEN.

"Murdered," Billy whispered as he reached out to trace the letters with his finger.

He touched the stone and there was a flash of blue light. A painful shock went through his body, forcing him to his knees. Sudden weakness shook him, and his eyes lost focus. He started to black out. At that instant, Billy heard angry voices from behind and with great effort managed to turn himself around.

A man and woman were arguing a few feet from him, near the pond, but their voices were muffled as if they were far away. The light was very dim to Billy's blurred vision. The man wore a broad sword at his side, and the woman's rich dress was that of a courtier, but he could make out little more than the couple's broader gestures and what appeared to be the sparkle of jewelry on both. The man bellowed as the lady knelt to plead with him. There was something very familiar about them both. Suddenly, the man struck the lady's face, knocking her down to the edge of the water. Raw anger coursed through Billy's veins, returning the energy to his limbs.

"Stop!" Billy leapt to his feet.

The man immediately knelt and grabbed the woman's throat. She vainly struggled against the warrior's superior strength. Billy bounded on to the bench and sprang at the man's back, but the man evaporated in his grasp, and Billy splashed face-first into the pond.

Billy jumped up in the shallow water of the pond and turned to face his opponent, but there was none. Neither the man nor the woman was anywhere to be seen. Rivulets of water ran down Billy's face and body. He shook his head to clear his vision and stumbled deeper into the pond. He swung around, first to his left, then to his right. He was alone in the garden.

"What just happened?" he muttered.

Billy felt a pain in his right arm and hand. He rubbed his forearm with his left hand and repeatedly flexed his fingers. *Must have hurt it when I landed.*

He waded out of the pond, leery of his surroundings. As he arrived on shore, he wrung out the bottom of his tunic and plopped down on the bench. When he was sure that he was absolutely alone, he took off his boots. As he watched the water pour out of them, he pondered what had just transpired.

"I must have been dreaming. Aye, that's it, I was sleepwalking." This seemed a satisfactory explanation until another thought occurred to him. *If that's true, how long was I sleepwalking? Did I dream the whole thing ... including Lady Myrredith and Sir Hugh? And how did I find my way here?* There were too many questions, and no answers. Billy scratched his head and looked at his wet attire.

"How am I gonna explain this one?" he asked a tiny bird, which had been watching him curiously from the thorn tree.

After Billy caught his breath, he got up and trudged towards the exit. By the time he reached the steps, he was in full stride, with a plan formulated to get his clothing dry and thus avoid having to explain their current state to Lady Myrredith. As he crossed the threshold into the donjon, he was halted midstride by a nagging echo in the back of his head. From the doorway, he turned around to look at the pond. The image of the woman being strangled still haunted him. The foreboding feeling returned, and Billy started to walk away. The sensation followed him like a soft, cold breath on the back of his neck. A shiver ran up his spine, spurring him into a gallop. Billy didn't stop running until he had cleared the main entrance of the donjon and was halfway to the kitchen.

* * *

Billy managed to avoid Lady Myrredith during the early morning, but he knew he would have to see her later, if not for his sake, then for hers. However, he still hadn't made up his mind about the king's offer and wanted to be alone to think. Lady Myrredith had done so much for him. It only felt right that he should stay with her and do whatever he could to repay her kindness. On the other hand, serving King William, in Castle Orgulous, even if he wasn't to be a knight, was a dream come true, and Lady Myrredith wanted him to accept. *Perhaps declining would be a greater break of faith with her than accepting.*

A voice broke into his thoughts. "My, but don't you look solemn."

Billy looked up. A lady stood just inches away with the sun over her shoulder. Billy's breath caught in his throat, and he fell backwards, for in the glare she looked like the woman he had seen strangled in the garden.

"I'm sorry." The lady moved closer. "I didn't mean to give you such a start."

As Billy's phantom moved, she eclipsed the sun, and he saw her face. "Princess Kathryn!"

The princess sat next to him. "What is it, William? You looked as if you'd seen a ghost."

"I thought I had."

"What?"

In that moment, an awful thought struck Billy. *What if it was Princess Kathryn I saw? But she's alive! Then it was ... the future ... and someone's going to kill her ... or try to!*

"What is the matter with you, William? Your eyes are as big as turnips."

"Your Highness." Billy spied about the courtyard. "You are in danger!"

"Danger?" the princess exclaimed.

"Yes, grave danger."

"Whatever are you talking about, William?"

"Someone will try to kill you. I don't know when, but I think soon."

"What? Here in Orgulous? Don't be ridiculous!"

Billy thought for a moment. Hugh had said that the queen was killed in Orgulous, right under the noses of the royal guard. He started to use this as an argument with the princess but then thought it better if she didn't know that he knew the truth. "I know it sounds impossible, but you must believe me."

"Oh, I see." Kathryn smiled as if she'd just grasped the punch line to a joke. "The assassins are everywhere. You must save me, Sir William!" she said melodramatically.

"No!" William wrinkled his forehead. "I'm not playing."

The princess concentrated on Billy. Something in his tone got his point across. "How do you know this?" she whispered.

"I saw ... I saw it happen. You must be careful!"

"What did you see, William?"

"I saw someone ... kill you."

Princess Kathryn laughed. "What?"

"In the garden!"

"But William, I'm here. I'm alive." She reached out and touched the back of her hand to Billy's forehead. "I think you must be ill."

"No! I saw it! I don't know how, but I saw it."

"William, were you dreaming, perhaps?"

"I—" Billy remembered that the very same thought had crossed his mind. "I guess ... maybe I had a ..."

"A nightmare?"

Billy nodded.

"I understand, William, sometimes dreams can seem very real indeed."

Billy nodded again, but his stomach was not convinced. There was something to the vision he had received, and he was certain that it wasn't wholly rooted in dreamland.

"So, my young friend, have you decided to stay with us? I know that my uncle and I will only be the better for it."

Billy fixed his eyes on at her. The idea of something happening to someone so beautiful and kind was more than he could stand—not to mention that she represented the future hopes of all Lyonesse. He knew no one would believe his story, and so he made his decision on the spot.

"Yes, I'm staying."

"Great! Does Myrredith know?"

"No, I just made up my mind."

"Then come. We must tell her immediately."

Princess Kathryn and Billy found Lady Myrredith in her room with Megan and Rhianna. They were packing the last of Myrredith's clothes for the journey home.

The two maids bowed in unison. "Your Highness."

Lady Myrredith turned round with a start. "Kathryn! Your Highness!"

"Myrredith."

Lady Myrredith spotted Billy. "William, where have you been?"

"Forgive me, milady, I had some thinkin' to do."

"Yes, of course, William. I understand."

Kathryn cut glances between Myrredith and her servants.

"Megan, Rhianna," Lady Myrredith said, "we can finish this later."

The servants bowed and left the room.

"What can I do for you, Your Highness?" Lady Myrredith asked.

Kathryn turned to Billy. "William ...?"

Myrredith observed Billy as he stared at his shuffling feet. "What is it, William?"

Billy continued to look at the floor as he answered his friend. He knew that if he looked at her his resolve would weaken, and he would not be able to tell her. "I made a decision. I am ... going ... to stay."

"That's wonderful, William!"

Billy looked up in surprise. He almost felt betrayed, but as his eyes met hers, he saw the pride she had in him and knew that it was for his sake that she was so pleased. Billy forced himself to smile, and then he ran to her and threw his arms around her waist.

"I'll leave you two alone," Kathryn said.

Billy turned to the princess. "No, please. Please stay."

"No, William, I should be elsewhere. After all, I've only been married one day. I don't want my husband to think I don't like him."

Kathryn stopped at the door. "Myrredith, please come to me later. We still have much to discuss."

"Yes, Your Highness."

Billy and Lady Myrredith bowed, and the princess left. They stood staring at each other, neither of them knowing what to say.

"I too have made a decision," Lady Myrredith said at last.

Billy sat down. "What is it?"

"When we first arrived here, I asked Princess Kathryn for a boon—a favor. She has agreed to grant my boon, and now I have decided that I should tell you what it is, although you can never tell anyone else."

Lady Myrredith crossed her arms and waited for Billy to affirm that he understood what she had said. Billy nodded and drew an X across his heart with his right index finger. Satisfied that this would hold his tongue, Lady Myrredith continued.

"As you know, Aonghas and I had no children. I am the last of the Cyndyn line. There is no Cyndyn heir. Now that he's gone, my boon becomes even more important." Lady Myrredith paused for a moment and knelt in front of Billy. She placed her hands on his and smiled. "When Kathryn sits on the throne, she has promised that her first official act will be to have your name placed on the Cyndyn family charter."

"I don't understand. What does it mean?"

"It makes you a Cyndyn. You would be my brother."

"Your brother?"

"Yes. You would be my family. My heir."

Billy was stunned. In all his life he had never met anyone like Lady Myrredith. People tended to treat him like some kind of freak, instead of a person. She not only treated him as a friend, she wanted him to be part of her family.

"Aren't you happy, William?"

"I-I don't know anything about being noble."

"On the contrary, I think you know more about being noble than many of those born to it."

"But I'm just an innkeeper's son."

"Not anymore. At least not after the princess takes the throne."

"I don't know what to say."

"Say nothing, William. I know your heart, and I know this is the right thing to do."

"But—"

"No buts, William! There's nothing to argue about. I've made up my mind. Do you understand?"

"Yes, Lady Myrredith." He knew that once she had her mind set on something, she was immovable.

"And furthermore, if you're to be my brother, I think you should call me

Myrredith, don't you?"

"Well, I ... I'll try. Maybe once it's official."

Lady Myrredith leaned forward and gave her brother-to-be a good squeeze. He hugged her in return, and she gave him a peck on the cheek.

"Oh, William. Later, when you come back to Cyndyn Hall, we will be so happy."

Billy released her. "What of my father?"

"He can stay with us too."

"He won't want to leave his inn."

"That's up to him." Lady Myrredith smiled. "You could always go visit him."

"Aye, I suppose so."

"Say, you better write your father another letter and tell him that you're staying here."

"Oh my goodness. I almost forgot."

"I'll take it with me when I leave." Lady Myrredith grinned. "Or you could ask Princess Kathryn to have a royal messenger deliver it!"

Billy's eyes grew large. "Could I?"

"Why not?"

"Maybe I had better do that. Otherwise, no one would ever believe."

* * *

Billy ate dinner with Lady Myrredith, then sat down to write his father while she visited the princess. It was difficult for Billy not to write anything about Lady Myrredith's boon, but it was harder still to tell his father that it would be even longer before they saw each other again. Billy wasn't sure how long he would be staying at Castle Orgulous, and that made him worry for his father. He began to have second thoughts about staying at all. Twice he had to start the letter over when the words he had written were spirited from the page by his tears. It was the most exhausting letter he had ever written, but at last it was finished. Billy carefully rolled up the letter and lay his head down on the table to rest. The next thing he knew, Megan was waking him for supper.

Billy stretched and looked up at her. "Where is Lady Myrredith?"

"She said to tell you she was dining with the princess."

"And Sir Hugh?"

"I don't know, dear, but you're welcome to eat with me and Rhianna."

"No, thank you, Megan. I think I should find Sir Hugh."

"Very well."

Billy searched throughout the donjon and as far as the stables, but he could not find Sir Hugh. He gave Splendore Pomponnel another piece of candy and started back. As he walked by the barracks for the second time, the smell of food tickled his nose and set off a bout of complaints from his stomach. He was famished, so he stopped in at the kitchen and charmed a plate of victuals from Dana, the hot-tempered Irish cook.

"I hear you'll be stayin' with us."

"For a while," Billy said between bites.

Dana's husband, Gryff, brought some gravy to the table and spooned it onto Billy's trencher. "Ya made quite an impression on the king."

"So I've been told."

Dana smiled. "I've never seen the man is such good spirits. Why, you'd think he was twenty years younger."

"Aye," Gryff said.

Billy looked up from his food. "I think it's Princess Kathryn's marriage."

Dana patted her husband's hand and pointed to a plate of fruit. "Oh sure, but we all seen his face when you were singin'."

Gryff grabbed an apple and brought it back to Billy. "I haven't seen the king that way since I was a boy."

"No one has." Dana leaned forward and whispered. "Not since the queen."

"What about the queen?" Billy asked.

Gryff sat down with his wife. "It's nothing boy. Just forget it."

Then Dana blurted out, in a husky whisper, "She was murdered."

"Quiet, woman!"

Billy's eyes widened. "You know about that?"

"Shh!" Dana hissed. "Strangled she was."

"Strangled?" mouthed Billy. The image of the woman being choked in his vision flashed in his head.

"Woman!" Gryff said in a warning tone that woke Billy from his trance.

Dana ignored him. "Aye, strangled. It were no drowning accident, as they'd have us believe." She then directed her words to her husband. "Most everyone here knows that!"

Gryff frowned. "Aye, but there's no sense in telling the boy."

"How do you know all this?" Billy was now whispering too.

"Gryff was just a young man at the time ..." Dana placed her hand on her man's. "But he saw."

Suddenly Gryff pushed back from his wife and stood. "I think you've said enough, woman!"

"What did ya see?" Billy asked earnestly. "I truly must know."

Dana stared up at her husband who was towering over her. He looked at Billy, measuring something in his mind. Slowly, he paced to the door, looked outside, and closed it. Then he turned to his wife and nodded. Dana was just about to speak when Gryff interrupted.

"But..." he said putting a well-callused finger on the end of Billy's nose, "but ya must first promise never to tell another living soul."

"I promise! I promise!"

Gryff withdrew his finger as Dana began to speak.

"As I was sayin', when Gryff was a young man—"

"Not that young."

Dana gave Gryff a dark look, then continued. "When he was younger, his parents served the king, much the way we do now. And like our little Mary, Gryff often helped with totin' food to and from the keep and here about. Wherever the nobles needed it."

"You're talking too much, woman! Just tell him before I change my mind."

"Be calm, husband. Billy's not gonna tell anyone, now are ya, love?"

"No ma'am."

"Ya see! Now as I was sayin', Gryff often brought food to the main keep. I think the queen was fond of him, and that's why he was sent to bring light refreshments to her in her garden every evenin'."

Gryff crossed his arms. "No, that's not why, but continue."

"Who's tellin' the story here?" Dana asked.

"I can't tell," said her husband. "It's taking so long!"

"Oh hush! I'm almost finished."

"You'd better be!"

Dana leaned closer to whisper. "Gryff was the one who found the queen."

"What?"

Gryff nodded sadly.

Billy wrinkled his brow. "And how did ya know it wasn't an accident?"

Dana deferred to her husband.

Gryff wrapped his fingers around his throat. "Marks. She had marks, here."

Again phantoms from Billy's vision invaded his head—images of the man putting his hands around the lady's throat. They ran in circles, shifting around and around through his mind.

"It wasn't a dream," William mumbled to himself.

"What, dear?" Dana asked.

"Huh? Oh, nothing. I was just talking to myself."

Billy got up and walked to the door without a word. The images intensified, pushing away his other thoughts.

"Where ya goin'?" Gryff asked.

Billy felt numb. "I don't know."

"Ya haven't finished your dinner, deary."

"Sorry, Dana. I'm not hungry anymore."

With that, Billy turned and wandered out into the ward. As he walked away, he heard Gryff fussing at his wife.

"Ya shouldn't have told him! Now look what you've done."

"What I've done?"

"At least you didn't mention the child ..."

Billy glanced back at the doorway. *I'm glad you told me.*

Their voices droned on and faded into garbled noise as Billy trudged across the inner ward to the donjon. His head was a storm of disturbing thoughts and violent images.

Billy roamed the halls of Castle Orgulous' main keep, searching for his companions and avoiding the area around the garden. Convinced that he had seen the queen's murder, he had no desire to go back there.

At last Billy found his friends in the company of Princess Kathryn and Prince Gaelyn, enjoying a quiet stroll through the inner ward. Billy was dying to tell them about his vision and find out more about the queen, but he was afraid that he would have to explain how he had come to the garden in the first place. The last thing he wanted was for his friends to find out about his spying on them.

"You're awfully quiet tonight, William," Lady Myrredith said as they entered the donjon.

"Oh, I-I'm just ..."

"Is there something you want to ask us?"

"No, Sir Hugh."

"Don't be sad, William," the princess said. "You will see Lady Myrredith and Sir Hugh again before long."

"And in the meantime," the prince added, "we would like ya to share our company."

"Thank you."

Myrredith bowed her head. "Yes, thank you, Your Highness. And now I think it's time that a certain young man went to bed."

Billy groaned. "You're always sending me to bed."

Myrredith grinned. "Well, we're just looking out for you."

"I wouldn't need looking out for if I were awake!"

The party of nobles laughed and said their goodnights to Billy. As he headed up the stairs, he turned and looked back at his four friends—two old and two new. Despite his father's warning about nobles, Billy found these four to be kind and agreeable. Seeing them all together, joined in friendship, warmed Billy. They were the future of Lyonesse, and from where Billy stood, that future looked great.

CHAPTER NINETEEN

Dark Days

The next morning, noble and commoner alike lined up along Lady Cyndyn's path from Castle Orgulous. Billy was amazed at how many came out to show their support of his patron. Dressed in black, they stood in solemn unity and bowed to her as she passed. Even the heavens were smeared with dark charcoal clouds. For the first time, Ergyfel seemed appropriately attired.

After Lady Myrredith and Princess Kathryn said their good-byes, Ergyfel approached. "Milady, the king sends his sympathies and wishes for a good journey."

"Thank you." Myrredith gave him a nod. "The king is not well?"

"No, milady," answered the King's First Counselor. "He was feeling less than himself this morning. The old sickness, I'm afraid."

"Yes. Please relay my wishes for His Majesty's speedy recovery."

"Of course, milady." Ergyfel bowed. As he rose, he made momentary eye contact with Billy. "Oh yes," he added with a smile, "don't worry about William, milady. I will keep an eye on the boy."

Before Myrredith could speak, Ergyfel stepped behind the wall of mourners. Billy watched him disappear into the sea of black. He noticed too that Lady Myrredith and Sir Hugh kept an eye on the magister. The lady's eyes were dark and hawklike as they pierced the crowd. The worry lines that Billy had come to know resurfaced. He took her hand.

The Earl of Hillshire appeared by her side. "Myrredith?"

She did not respond.

"Myrredith?"

"Yes. Oh, Finney! Please forgive me."

"Of course, my dear."

"I wish you were coming with us, old friend," Myrredith said.

"I am."

"What?"

"Why yes," the earl said. "I can't imagine not being there for you when you arrive at Waru-Dunom."

"But the coronation!"

"I would only be bored into unconsciousness—a condition someone of my advanced years views with apprehension."

Lady Myrredith bowed to Earl Finney. "My deepest gratitude."

"No, no, no." The earl offered a hand to Myrredith. "None of that now, child. We are too long friends and I am too old for all that nonsense. Now let us be off. I insist that you ride with me, at least for the first part of our journey."

"Yes, of course, Finney."

Malcolm helped the Earl of Hillshire and Lady Myrredith up into their wagon, then climbed into the one behind it. Billy hated to see his juggling master leave but decided, as did Malcolm, that Lady Myrredith needed his company more than anyone in Orgulous.

Even though Billy and Lady Myrredith had said their farewells a dozen times that morning, neither one of them wanted their separation to begin. They had hardly been apart since their acquaintance, and now it felt like the end. It felt wrong.

As the wagon started to roll away, Lady Myrredith repeated what she had told Billy earlier, concerning proper behavior. Billy trotted along beside them as they exited the giant gateway of the castle.

"And obey Princess Kathryn, and Prince Gaelyn, and—"

"I'll be good." Billy crossed his heart.

Lady Myrredith stopped lecturing and smiled. "I know you will. When we return, you must tell me everything about the coronation!"

"I'll pay extra close attention, so I don't miss anything!"

Lady Myrredith began to tear up, and so Billy jumped into the moving wagon. Lady Myrredith threw her arms around him and squeezed. Billy wished she would just keep holding him.

"Take care, little brother," she whispered.

Billy felt the wetness of her tears on his cheek. "You too, Myrredith."

Billy felt his heart breaking as the wagon slowed to a stop. Sir Hugh dismounted and helped him down from the wagon. The two of them stood silently, then Billy stretched out his hand. Hugh clasped his forearm in the manner Billy had seen him greet other knights.

"Thanks, Sir Hugh ... for everything."

"Thank you."

Hugh tousled Billy's hair, then handed him Splendore Pomponnel's reins while he mounted. The spirited horse snorted and gave Billy a friendly nudge with its nose. Billy pulled out the last piece of sugar candy from his pocket and gave it to Splendore.

"I'll miss you too, Splendore."

The entire party moved out as Sir Hugh took control of the willful horse and turned him alongside the wagon. An ache grew in Billy's chest with each wagon that rolled by, leaving him behind.

As Billy stood in the road, watching Hugh and Myrredith disappear from sight, he had the feeling that this was more than just a good-bye. Much like the first time they met, he simply knew that they were to be friends, and now he felt as if they might never see each other again.

Billy waited for the last wagon to leave his sight then turned and plodded back to Castle Orgulous. As he reached the Gleaming Gate, a boy ran past him carrying a large black bag.

"Hey, stop! What's the hurry?" Billy ran to catch him.

"I can't stop," the boy said. "My master needs these medicines now!"

"Your master?"

"Aye. My master is Dhwen, the king's physician."

"King William's physician?"

"Aye."

"The king is sick?"

"Very!"

Billy kept step with the physician's apprentice. "I better go too. I'm the king's new court musician."

"The new jester?"

"Musician!"

"As you wish. My name is James."

"I'm Billy."

"I know."

"You do?"

"Yes. I was at the wedding feast."

"Oh."

The boys were too out of breath to say anything more. Panting, they made their way up the donjon's many flights of stairs, upsetting several nobles and surprising guards. James went straight to the king's chamber while Billy went to collect his lute.

Princess Kathryn had arranged for Billy to have a room near her own. It was not as spacious as the one he had in Lady Myrredith's suite, but he didn't plan to spend much time there. Billy popped into his room only long enough to grab his instrument and then darted down the long hallway to the king's chambers.

Two guards stopped Billy as he approached the T-intersection before the royal suite. James was nowhere to be seen, but Billy heard him from behind the large oaken door.

"Halt!" the guards said, as Billy went for the door.

Billy stopped and stared at them. "But I'm the king's new musician!"

"You haven't been summoned," said the guard on the left.

"But—"

"You'll just have to wait," said the guard on the right.

Billy realized that it wasn't any use to argue, so he looked around for a place to sit. Down the hall, to his left, he found a small ledge with a narrow window. The view from the window gave him chills. It was the Queen's Garden. Billy turned his back to the window and waited.

After what felt like an eternity for Billy, Ergyfel arrived. He dismissed the guards and walked directly into the king's suite. It seemed odd that he should dismiss the guards, *but then again, he is the King's First Counselor.*

Billy listened intently, trying to hear what was being said, but the door was too thick. Suddenly the door swung open, and James appeared. He stood in the doorway as a thin voice from within gave him instructions.

"And come back soon with that water. I may need you to fetch more medicine from the apothecary."

James nodded. "Yes, master."

Billy approached the door. As James turned to leave, he saw Billy coming and stopped for a moment, leaving the door ajar.

"How's the king?"

"He's not well."

"Why aren't you in there with your master?"

"The magister told him to send me away."

"Why?"

"I don't know. Maybe he needs to discuss something with the king in private."

Billy looked over James's shoulder into the room and could see the old physician talking. He was a grey-bearded man, dressed in plain brown clothing with the sleeves of his shirt rolled up to his elbows. Upon his bald head, he wore a small blue hat with a red ribbon in the back. Billy noticed tiny drops of blood on the front of his shirt. In his hands he carried a small bowl.

"I better go," James said. "He'll need that water before long."

Billy watched the young apprentice run down the hallway, then turned his attention back to the door. Dhwen, the physician, was still standing where Billy could see him.

Dhwen raised his voice. "But they're dead!"

"What do you mean?" Ergyfel asked.

The physician picked something small and black out of the bowl using tongs. He held the object up in the air and let it drop into the bowl, then picked up another. He repeated this as he continued.

"The leeches are all dead! I think you should do something!"

"What do you mean, Dhwen? What are you saying?"

"The king is poisoned!"

"What?"

Poisoned? Billy clamped a hand over his mouth.

"Yes," Dhwen said. "I've never seen its like, but I can tell you most other men would be dead by now. The king has always had a very strong will, even through these many years of sickness. It's the only thing keeping him alive."

"Only his will ... What should we do?"

"I'm afraid it is beyond my skills, Magister, but if you were to ... do something ..."

"Do what, physician?"

"Who could condemn you for using your powers to save our king?"

"Powers?"

"I would not mention it if not for—"

"Believe me, Doctor, I have done everything I can. And you ... you have done everything you can."

"I ... have done everything I can."

Dhwen's posture relaxed. Then Ergyfel's voice changed subtly, taking on a smooth, sonorous tone.

"There's nothing more to be said."

"Nothing more to be said," the physician repeated.

"That's right, Dhwen. There's no need to mention the poison."

"No poison."

"And no leeches. The king will recover, with rest."

"No leeches. The king will recover."

"That's right. We don't want to unduly worry or alarm the princess."

"No, no worry."

"Good. Remember that, and everything will be fine."

Suddenly the old physician crumpled, just catching himself before he fell to the floor.

"Are you well, Doctor?"

"Oh … yes, thank you." The king's physician was shaking. "Just a little spell, nothing to worry about. You see, when you reach my age—"

"I hope it's not the same as the king."

"The king? Oh yes, the king! No, no. I'm just an old man, but the king will recover. He just needs rest."

"Good. I'm glad to hear that, Dhwen. Now I must leave, and you must take care of your patient."

"Yes, quite so."

Billy turned and scuttled away from the door. Before he could make the corner, he heard the door groan behind him, and he made an about-face. Ergyfel came through the door and strutted down the hallway.

"William, what brings you here?"

"I thought the king might wish to hear some music. Maybe it would make him feel better."

"His physician is with him right now. He says we should allow the king to rest."

"Oh. How is the king?"

"His Majesty is fine, nothing to worry about. Perhaps you should find the princess. I'm sure she would like to hear some of your music."

"Yes, I think I will."

Billy immediately sought out the princess. He didn't have to look far, as she was in her suite. Arlyn, the guard stationed at the door, knocked, and a maid allowed Billy into the central chamber. It was not unlike the suite Billy had shared with Lady Myrredith.

The princess entered the room. "William, what a pleasant surprise."

"I'm sorry, Your Highness, but I had to see you."

"Do you miss Lady Myrredith already?"

Billy's mind was concerned with more pressing subjects, but the mention of his friend sent a pang through him. "Yes. I missed her before she left."

"Oh, William!" The princess laughed. "Do not fret. You will see her before long. I see you have brought your lute. Would you like to play for me?"

"Yes, Your Highness, but that's not why I came to see you."

"Oh? What is it?"

"May I speak with you alone?"

Princess Kathryn nodded to her maid. The servant bowed and left quietly to the next room. As soon as the door was closed, Billy started.

"Your Highness, I know something very important."

The princess stepped closer. "What is it? Why are we whispering?"

"Because I don't want anyone to hear."

"Hear what?"

"The king has been poisoned."

"What?" the princess shouted.

"Shhh!" Billy hissed.

Immediately the door to the next room flew open, and in charged Gwyn. She sent a searing glance at Billy and then looked to her mistress.

"Is everything well, Your Highness?"

The princess looked at Billy and her maid. A smile crossed her face.

"Yes, everything is fine, Gwyn."

"Yes, Your Highness." The maid bowed and retreated into the adjoining room.

"William," Kathryn started, "you really shouldn't play games like that. With my uncle's health being what it is, you nearly scared me to death."

"I'm not playing! You must believe me!"

Billy had a sinking feeling after he spoke, as he remembered saying those exact words to the princess before. When he tried to warn her of what he thought would be an attempt on her life, she believed he was playing or fevered. Now she would believe he was making it up.

The princess watched Billy's expression as he struggled to puzzle out his dilemma. She leaned forward and pushed the hair away from his frowning face.

"It's very important to you, isn't it?"

Billy didn't respond.

"Very well! Who's our evil culprit? The Irish? The Welsh? Maybe the Saxons. Oh, I know, someone inside the castle, right?"

Billy did not know how to respond. He didn't want to prolong the idea that this was some product of his imagination.

"Yes," Billy answered at last, "but—"

"Is it Ambassador Snegaddrick?"

"No. It's not like that."

"Like what?"

"It's not what you think."

"What do you mean? It's someone outside the castle?"

"No! I didn't imagine it!"

"What? What didn't you imagine?"

"It's—" Billy stopped short of saying the name out loud. He looked cautiously about the room and then whispered. "It's the magister."

Princess Kathryn stepped back from Billy. She cocked her head to one side and eyed him carefully. Then she knelt in front of him.

"William," she said with a stern expression, "this is a game, right?"

Billy started to cry tears of frustration. He looked away from her to hide his tears.

"Tell me, William." The princess gently turning his head. "Everything will be fine." She placed her hands on his shoulders. "I didn't mean to upset you, but the kind of games you want to play are too-too serious, if you know what I mean."

Billy pulled away from her. "This is the truth!" Sudden inspiration shot through him. "And I can prove it!" He ran for the door.

"Prove it?" The princess stood up to follow him.

"The leeches! The leeches are my proof!"

Without another word, Billy fled from the princess' room and down the hallway towards the king's chambers. Kathryn gave chase, asking the guard to come with her. When Billy arrived, the two guards were again stationed on either side of the door. Dhwen was leaving with his apprentice.

"Dhwen!" Billy spouted. "You must show Princess Kathryn the leeches!"

The physician stepped back from Billy. "Who are you?"

"I am Billy, the king's new musician."

"Jester, hunh? I have no time for jests."

"No!" Billy insisted. "This is not a jest."

At that moment, Princess Kathryn and Arlyn came around the corner.

"Your Highness," the physician said with a respectful bow. "Is there anything I can do for you?"

"How is my uncle?"

"He is resting now. He will recover, but he needs his rest. There's nothing more to say."

"What about the leeches?" Billy asked.

The physician looked curiously at Billy and frowned. "I have no leeches, boy."

"But the king—"

"The king has no need for bleeding. Everything will be fine."

Billy noticed James shuffling his feet anxiously.

Kathryn glanced at Billy. "No poison then?"

"Poison?" the physician and Arlyn said in unison.

Dhwen continued. "Good heavens no, Your Highness! I'm afraid this boy has unduly alarmed you. The king will recover. I've done all that I can. There's nothing more to say."

Billy frowned. *The exact same words. He must be under a spell!* He quickly turned to James. "He used leeches on the king, didn't he?"

James stepped back and started to fidget. "Well, I-I thought ... I thought maybe ..."

Dhwen gave the boy a searing look. "You thought what?"

"Nothing, master."

"Quite right, you oaf!" The old physician turned to the princess and bowed again. "My apologies, Your Highness. These two rumormongers have obviously been playing some sort of game. Now if you will excuse us, I have patients elsewhere who require my attention."

"Yes, of course."

Dhwen bowed and then grabbed James by the ear and escorted him down the hall. "And if you wish to remain my apprentice, you will keep your mouth shut and stop gossiping like some scullery maid. There are many who would appreciate your position!"

"Yes, master," James said, taking a kick to his rear.

Billy's hopes for the truth unraveled as he watched them leave. Then his eyes moved to the princess, who stood with her hands on her hips—looking very much like Lady Myrredith.

"I'm sorry." Billy hung his head. In truth Billy was apologizing for his failure, not for any inconvenience.

"William, what am I to do with you?"

Billy shrugged and kicked at the floor.

"You've got to get a hold on that imagination of yours, or it will be your undoing. Why don't you go to your room for a while?"

Billy's head was churning as the princess took him back to his room. *Maybe I could convince someone else. Perhaps Dana and Gryff will believe me. But they're only cooks, what good would that do? I need someone big, like ... Prince Gaelyn!*

As Billy turned it over in his mind, he became convinced that somehow he would have to get the truth out of the physician. James was obviously too unsure or afraid, and he wouldn't dare confront Ergyfel. Any remaining doubt that Ergyfel was practicing magic had evaporated with Dhwen's performance.

How can I possibly fight Ergyfel's sorcery?

Billy scratched his head as he paced the length of his room. It was an impossible task. And though it frightened him, he was determined to do it.

"There must to be a way," he said, thinking aloud. "I've got to break the spell." Billy looked down at his lute and his juggling gear. "Oh! I don't know anything about magic. I'm a musician, not a magician."

A new idea struck Billy without warning. An idea so daring and devious that it brought him chills of delight.

I'll get the magister to break his own spell. All I have to do ... is convince him that his spell has failed. He'll drop whatever he's doing in order to fix it. That's when we'll nab him! But first ...

"I better get some help."

Billy was excused immediately after dinner when he explained that Lady Myrredith's absence and the king's illness had upset him. He left the royal couple and went directly to the kitchen. It didn't take long for Billy to convince Dana and Gryff that Ergyfel was poisoning the king.

"That no-good, connivin' backstabber." Gryff spit on the ground. "He's been nothin' but trouble from the day he arrived!"

"Aye, husband, but what can we do about it?"

"Aye, what?"

Billy grinned impishly. "I have an idea on that."

Gryff scowled at him. "I don't like the look on your face, laddie. I don't like it a bit, but I'm listenin'."

Late into the night, Gryff and Dana listened as Billy laid out his plan to trap the King's First Counselor. Several times they started to walk out, claiming that the whole idea was too flimsy and dangerous, but each time

Billy managed to persuade them to hear him out. In the end, Billy won them over, and together they agreed to launch the plan on the morrow.

The night crept by for Billy. He couldn't sleep with his head so packed with intrigue. He mulled over the events of the day and the steps of his plan—looking for things that would need special attention. At last, completely exhausted, Billy nodded off.

Billy awoke to a scream: his own. As he shakily turned up the lamp wick next to his bed, the door crashed open under the weight of a guardsman. Billy jumped back, bumping his head against the wall. Billy and the guard had carefully scrutinized each other from top to bottom when Princess Kathryn and Prince Gaelyn showed up at the door with a half-dozen guards.

"What are you doing standing on the bed, William?" Princess Kathryn demanded. "This is no time for games!"

Billy rubbed his head and pointed at the guardsman. "He broke down my door and scared me half to death!"

The prince and princess looked at the guard and asked, "Why did you break down the door?"

The guard looked confused as to whom he should answer then turned to Kathryn. "I heard a scream, Your Highness."

"Why did you scream, William?"

At that moment, more guards showed up and greeted their comrades. Billy looked at the crowd staring at him in his nightclothes and felt very exposed. He stepped off the bed and pulled a blanket around himself.

"Why did you scream?" Kathryn repeated.

Billy looked away from her very sheepishly. "I had a bad dream."

"A bad dream?" the first guard said. Then he quickly turned to the princess. "Please pardon me, Your Highness."

"No harm done. Very understandable." Kathryn turned to the other guards. "Well, I think we've had enough excitement for one night. Thank you, men. That will be all." As the men left, she turned to Gaelyn.

"Husband, I think you should return to bed. I'll follow, as soon as I finish with William."

"Very well, my dearest. Good night, William. See you on the morrow."

Once they were alone, Princess Kathryn tucked Billy into his bed. She sat with him while he told her about his nightmare.

"Then, when Sir Hugh came out of the dragon—like all the times before—he turned on me! He was trying to kill me!"

"Now, William, you know as well as I do that Hugh would never do anything to harm you."

"I know, but just the same it happened."

"In your dream."

"Aye."

"You've dreamt this same dream before?"

"Aye, except Hugh was always my friend after he killed the dragon."

"Well, you shouldn't think any more about it."

Kathryn kissed Billy on the forehead. Then she pulled away from him and made a queer face.

"What is it, Your Highness?"

"For a moment, you looked just like—" Princess Kathryn shook her head. "It's nothing. You know, this afternoon I was quite angry with you, and now ... I guess you've been through much, William. I'm sorry."

With that said, the princess started to turn down the lamp. Billy reached out and gently touched her arm.

"Please don't, Your Highness."

"Yes, of course." She turned up the lamp. "Good night."

"Good night, Your Highness. Thank you."

The princess stopped in the doorway. "Sweet dreams, William. I'll have someone fix this door tomorrow."

Billy spent the rest of the night tossing and turning and found only a smidgen of the sleep he had lost.

* * *

In the days that followed, Dana and Gryff carefully seeded the rumor mill. According to their "reliable source," the king's physician, while in a drunken stupor at a local establishment, let slip about his royal patient's poisoning. At first they told only those servants known to be fairly close lipped, but later they served up morsels of the story with each platter carried from their kitchen. Thanks to Arlyn, the rumor of poison would already be making its rounds through the guards. It was only a matter of time before Ergyfel's informants would bring him the rumor.

Billy maintained a low profile to regain the confidence of the princess and prince. He sang and juggled for them when they requested, but slipped away to keep an eye on the magister whenever possible. After a few days of this observation, Billy became aware of others in Castle Orgulous who were keeping an eye on Ergyfel. Most were frightened, some hateful, a few curious, and one admiring. Billy marked them well, especially the Lady Maeven, whose stare lingered a little too long on the King's First Counselor.

Billy made mental lists of all the players in the drama unfolding at Castle Orgulous. It was important to know who could be counted on for what, but the most vital figure of all was the one that was still missing. Billy needed someone of bearing, a witness beyond Ergyfel's reach, to be present when he sprung the trap. The trick was in the timing. Knowing when Ergyfel would make his move wasn't good enough; Billy had to force the magister to move when the trap was set.

During this time, Billy was also getting to know Prince Gaelyn. Any reservations Billy might have felt about this royal foreigner he soon forgot, and they became fast friends. The prince taught Billy how to play chess and Gwythian-style horse riding, and Billy taught the prince songs from Lyonesse. They were seldom seen apart in Castle Orgulous and were most often sharing a laugh. Behind his back, Billy's nickname became "the prince's pet."

Prince Gaelyn held himself up on a crenel in the curtain wall. "You really are too much!"

Billy smiled. "Thank you ... I think."

Gaelyn laughed again and then finally got a hold on himself. He looked at his youthful companion and smiled appreciatively.

"I really am lucky, William."

"Why?"

"Because I have found somethin' here in Lyonesse that I never dreamt possible."

"What's that?"

Gaelyn looked from the battlements to the green hills surrounding Nyraval. "I have made many friends here, when I expected to find myself surrounded by begrudgin' enemies. In truth, I have found more friends right here, than in all sixteen cities of Caertref y Gwlad."

"Where?"

"Caertref y Gwlad is the island you call Gwythia. But best of all, I have found two very special friends, in you and Kathryn. I do not think ya can know what trepidation I felt when I found that I was to be married off to a woman I had never met or even seen! Moreover, I was to live in a land away from my home and family. The ambassadors started inflating me with glowin' reports of Kathryn, even before our voyage here. By the time we sighted Tintagel, I was convinced that I was being saddled with a boorish, spoiled, homely, domineerin' foreigner, with no respect or understandin' of our ways or me. I nearly jumped ship! I'm happy I didn't do that!"

Prince Gaelyn paused again, deep in thought. Suddenly, he spoke with great emotion and tenderness. "I find Kathryn witty, spirited, and more beautiful than I could have ever imagined." Then in a voice barely above a whisper he added, "And I am hopelessly in love with her."

"She is in love with you too."

Gaelyn looked at him. "Do ya really think so?"

"I know so. She said to me just yesterday, that you two are as one. That together, you would make Lyonesse a wonderful place to live again."

Prince Gaelyn smiled. "Yes, we both share that same dream."

"Dreams are important."

"Aye. Perhaps the most important thing of all."

They continued their walk along the battlements in silence. While the prince's company helped take Billy's mind off Lady Myrredith and Sir Hugh, his thoughts were seldom far from Ergyfel. Billy tried to decipher what Ergyfel hoped to achieve by murdering the king. *Was he the man who killed the queen?* If he wanted the throne—Princess Kathryn was now the heir apparent and would be crowned in mere days—the throne was out of his reach, unless ...

He can't be planning to kill her too! There's no way he could get away with it ... is there?

Ambassador Snegaddrick appeared and pulled Prince Gaelyn aside. The snobbish statesman glared down his nose at Billy, at last cocking his "get lost" eyebrow as a warning. Billy bowed to the prince, then left to wander and ponder alone.

As Billy mulled over the horrible possibilities of Ergyfel's plans, a servant he had marked as one of the magister's informants approached him. Billy had only seen the man speaking with the First Counselor and the other servants, and so he was caught completely off guard when the man spoke to him.

"Why so glum, Jester?"

"What?"

"Why so glum?"

"Oh, um ... I'm just worried about the king."

"Then you've heard?" the servant whispered.

"Heard what?"

"About the poisonin'," the man hissed. "Some says it was spies from Gwythia. But don't you worry none, it's probably just rumor."

"Aye ... a rumor."

"Besides, Lord Ergyfel just told me he'd be lookin' into it."

Billy was again completely shocked. Finding out when Ergyfel had heard the rumor was supposed to be the hard part of his plan.

The servant turned to walk away. "Well, gotta run."

Billy scurried after him. "Wait. Did ya hear anything more?"

The servant continued to walk as he chatted to Billy. "Naw. I only just heard meself ... Bodach says he saw a demon fly in the king's window night before last, but everyone knowed Bodach visits the king's wine cellar much too often."

"Who started the rumor?"

The servant shrugged. "Who knows? Nobody really knows who starts a rumor. That's what makes it a rumor now, don't it? The juicy ones anyhow. Well, like to work me jaw all day, but I don't have time now." The man stepped up his pace and left Billy behind.

Billy stopped by the kitchen to give Dana and Gryff an update and tell them to prepare for the next stage. The sky was darkening with storm clouds as he returned to the donjon in search of Lady Maeven.

Billy located Maeven amongst the same giggling, gossiping gaggle of ladies he had seen her with his first day in Castle Orgulous. Their constant chatter and giggling reminded Billy of spooked chickens.

"Lady Maeven?" Billy said from a timid distance.

The ladies all turned and stared at him. Then amid hushed whispers and giggles, the lady was prodded from their midst by the others.

"I am Maeven," she said with a nod, "daughter of Sir Feolaghe."

Billy bowed to her, and the giggling increased.

"What do you want, jester?"

Billy bit back his pride. "Might I speak to you privately?"

Maeven looked back at her snickering friends before warily stepping away from them. Billy kept his distance until they were well out of the hearing range of the others.

"Well?" she demanded.

"I have some very important information that must reach the King's First Counselor."

"Why not tell him yourself?"

"He doesn't like me."

"And you think he'll like me?"

Billy looked her in the eye.

"Why ask me?"

"I know you ... have an eye for the magister."

Her face turned red. "Who said that?"

"I have eyes too, milady. I have noticed the way you look at him."

Maeven blushed even more. She turned away from Billy, attempting to hide her face.

"If I am wrong, milady, I am most sorry."

Maeven was quiet. Billy bit his lip and crossed his fingers.

"You are very perceptive," she said at last. Then, without turning back to Billy she asked, "What is this information?"

Billy calculated his next words very carefully. He knew that if he appeared too eager she might not trust him.

"Are you sure, milady?"

"Yes."

"It's just that now I'm not so sure you're the right one."

"Go ahead. I will tell Ergyfel."

"Very well." Billy nervously scanned the ward. "The king ... has been poisoned."

"What?" Maeven, turning around to face Billy. "You think that's news? You fool! You jester! Is this a joke? I heard that rumor two days ago, from my maid!"

"Ah," Billy said apologetically. "Then you already know about Dhwen and everything?"

"Dhwen? The physician?"

"Aye."

"What about him?"

"Ya probably already heard."

"Heard what?"

"That Dhwen knows who did it."

Maeven was suddenly silent, and uncharacteristically so for a long while. Billy waited for her response.

"Who?" she asked at last.

"Who?"

"Who did it, you fool?"

"I don't know! I only heard that Dhwen knows."

"And why hasn't he done something?"

"How should I know? Maybe he's scared or somethin'."

"Of what?"

"Look," Billy said, "I don't know, but I'm getting a little scared myself. Good day, milady."

Billy turned and hurried away from Maeven. As he rounded the corner, he looked over his shoulder to watch her. Maeven's friends called to her, but she paid them no heed. Instead, she straightened her dress and walked in a direction Billy felt sure she would find Ergyfel.

* * *

Billy knocked on the door to the chambers of the prince and princess. The door opened, and Gwyn stuck her head out into the hallway.

"Oh, it's you," she declared. "I suppose you'll be wantin' to see Prince Gaelyn then?"

"Yes, please."

Gwyn sighed and rolled her eyes. "Very well."

Billy slipped by her as she opened the door. "Thank ya, mum."

"Well, at least you've got *some* manners."

"Thank ya, mum."

Billy found Prince Gaelyn sitting on his balcony. The newlywed was preoccupied with a stack of letters that covered the small table near his side.

"Good afternoon, Your Highness."

The prince continued to stare at the papers. "Good afternoon."

"I'm sorry to disturb you, Your Highness..."

Gaelyn glanced up to Billy and then back to his papers. "What is it, William?"

Billy had never seen the prince so serious. Since the beginning of their friendship, Prince Gaelyn had always greeted Billy with a smile. "Is there a problem, Your Highness?"

"No. Not a problem. Snegaddrick just delivered these letters from Father."

"I don't like that man," Billy said, half to himself.

"My father?"

"No, no. I've never met him. It's ambassador Snegaddrick I don't care for."

"Aye, he can be a bit paughty."

"Is everything well in Gwythia, Your Highness?"

"Yes, yes. My father just wishes to seal the treaty between our two nations."

"That's great! Isn't it?"

"Yes, of course." Gaelyn laughed. "Ya know, William, I envy you."

"Me?"

"Yes, my friend. Ya really haven't any idea about these things, have ya?"

"What things?"

"Exactly!"

Prince Gaelyn let out another laugh. Billy liked the sound of his laughter. He never laughed at cruelty or misfortune and rarely, if ever, held back. He was, in Billy's words, "an honest laugher."

At that moment, Princess Kathryn appeared behind Billy. "William, I knew it had to be you."

He turned to face her. "What, Your Highness? What had to be me?"

"I heard my husband laughing, and I knew that you had arrived."

"Tis true enough, William," the prince said. "My dear wife has been trying to make me laugh all morning—"

"After you received those letters."

"And now, William, you have succeeded where she could not."

"That doesn't surprise me," Kathryn said.

"I'm sorry, Your Highness," Billy said with a bow.

Both royals laughed again.

"William," the princess said, between laughs, "you really are a treasure! Now, what can we do for you?"

The prince sat up. "Did ya come to brighten up this dismal day with a song?"

"Or dazzle us with another juggling trick?"

"Or better me in another rousing game of chess?"

"Oh no, Your Highnesses," Billy said apologetically. "I'm sorry, but I only came to ask Prince Gaelyn if he would meet me later this evening."

Gaelyn raised an eyebrow. "Meet ya?"

"Aye. I want to show ya somethin'."

"What?"

"Um … It's a surprise."

"Can I see it too?" Kathryn asked.

Billy turned to her. "I'm sorry, Your Highness, but this is—um—men stuff."

"Men stuff?" Princess Kathryn laughed. "Very well, *men*. After the surprise, I will expect you here for dinner."

"Yes, Your Highness." Billy bowed his head. He then turned and started to leave. "I'll bring my lute for ya then."

The princess put her hands together. "Wonderful!"

"Beloved, what about Ergyfel's feast?"

Kathryn gave her husband a surprised expression. "I didn't think you were interested in going. He's only hosting a feast to draw attention away from our coronation. What's more, he only invited us because he knew I wouldn't accept."

"Maybe we should spoil his fun and go anyway," Gaelyn quipped.

"Don't be ridiculous," his wife reposted. "If the magister has invited everyone to a feast, at his expense, you can bet he's up to no good. I only hope he doesn't poison them all."

The prince and princess laughed, but with what he knew, Billy didn't find it at all humorous. He smiled to cover his apprehension.

"At any rate, I have planned a splendid feast for us in a more private dining hall."

"Sounds great," said Gaelyn.

"Aye," Billy agreed, as he turned to leave.

"Where shall I meet ya, William?" the prince asked.

Billy did an about-face. "Hunh?"

"The surprise. Remember?"

Billy turned pale. "Oh, I almost forgot! It's very important ya meet me on the bailey wall, near the repairs, just before dusk."

"Oo-oo-oo" mouthed the prince. "Sounds mysterious and intriguing. I look forward to an interesting surprise."

"I promise, you won't be disappointed."

Billy left and went immediately to the bailey wall to check on his preparations. Over the last two days he had managed to set up a small hiding place amid the construction materials on the wall. There, Prince Gaelyn and he would stay hidden from sight, to witness what transpired between the King's First Counselor and the king's physician. If everything went according to plan, Prince Gaelyn would have Ergyfel placed under arrest that night.

Billy arrived at the wall but felt strangely, as if someone was watching him. He scanned the inner ward and outer walls, but hardly a soul was present. A light drizzle had driven most everyone indoors. Only a few servants and guards scurried about or stood watch, and none of them paid him any attention.

A flash of movement caught Billy's eye, and he followed it to the high hill just south of Castle Orgulous. Large, dark boulders sprouted from the top of the hill, standing in a circle where some long forgotten people had placed them. To Billy, they looked like a band of knights warming themselves around a fire.

Just then, a pale horse roamed into view between the rocks and then disappeared again. Billy focused on the distant hilltop, trying to catch another glimpse of the creature in the dismal light. He was rewarded with a flash of white between the dark stones, and then another. A moment later, the beast appeared in whole beside the ancient monument, wrapped in black barding and carrying a black-clad rider on its back. Billy's heart skipped a beat. It was the same woman he had seen at Cyndyn Hall—it was the Night Queen! There was no mistaking that strange black armor and owl-like helm.

As she had done at Cyndyn Hall, the Night Queen froze and stared at Billy. Even from her distant perch, he could feel her alien purple eyes beating down on him. Her spirited horse strutted in a tight circle before she reined it back to face Orgulous. Then, without warning, she turned her mount and disappeared into the large standing stones.

Billy scanned the hilltop for several minutes, but the Night Queen never emerged again. Then he remembered why he was on the bailey wall and quickly returned to his preparations.

After some last minute adjustments to his hiding place, Billy hopped into an empty barrel and waited for Prince Gaelyn. The heavy black thunderclouds overhead, which had only delivered a light sprinkle, began to make good on their threat.

Billy pulled a tarp over the top of his barrel. *What if Dhwen or Ergyfel doesn't show up? This stupid rain could ruin everything! And seeing the Night Queen here is surely a bad omen.*

The dark clouds made it difficult to tell what time it was, but Billy knew that it was nearing dusk. The critical time for Billy's plan would soon be upon him, and still there was no sign of Prince Gaelyn.

"Where could he be?" Billy said, thinking aloud. "He should have been here by now!"

There was a crash of thunder and then another. The storm was worsening. In the next flash of lightning, Billy saw the lone figure of Dhwen climbing the steps at the far end of the wall. He wore an oiled leather cloak wrapped tightly around him and carried his black bag.

Where is Gaelyn?

Slowly the healer crossed the wall, squinting and wiping the rain from his face. He stopped and set down his bag on the jagged stones of the broken wall. Billy could see him clearly as he was now a mere fifteen feet away. Dhwen pulled his cloak closer around himself; there was another stroke of lightning, and suddenly a dark figure appeared in front of him. Billy's breath caught in his chest, and the old man stumbled back in surprise.

"Magister!"

"Yes, Dhwen, it is I."

Billy recognized Ergyfel's sonorous voice and wanted to scream. Half of his instincts urged him to leap out of the barrel, while the other half held him fast. It was sheer torture. The prince hadn't shown, and now it was too late!

What should I do?

"Magister." The physician's voice was quaking. "What can I do for you?"

"Why are you shaking, Dhwen?"

"It's cold."

"I think you're frightened, Dhwen. Are you frightened?"

"I-I ..."

Billy watched as the grey-bearded doctor cowered before the younger man, who was the king's cousin. He looked like a repentant younger sibling preparing to receive a beating.

"Are you hiding something from me, Dhwen?"

"Hiding? Good heavens no, Magister! I would never hide anything from you."

"Is that so?"

Dhwen's eyes darted around. "How is the king?"

Ergyfel crossed his arms. "Why don't you tell me?"

"The king is sick. He's been sick for a long time now."

"But I hear you've been saying something ... more."

"I don't know what you mean."

"Come now, Doctor, no need to lie about it. You know that eventually I hear everything."

"I'm not lying!" Dhwen took a step back from Ergyfel. "I don't know what you're talking about."

"You were the only one who knew about the poison, Dhwen. What I don't understand is how you managed to break my spell."

"Poison? Spell?"

Like the lightning, Ergyfel snapped out and grabbed the elderly physician by his throat. "Was it the faerie?" he demanded, pushing Dhwen closer to the edge of the crumbling wall.

Billy felt a surge of adrenaline, but it only made his chest muscles tighten unbearably. Dhwen grabbed the magister's wrist with both hands and tried to pry his hand away. His eyes became feral as he looked at the ground far below his precarious footing.

"I'll repeat my question." Ergyfel forced Dhwen further over the precipice. "Was it the faerie? Was it Billy?"

"Stop! Please!"

"Have it your way. Your secret dies with you."

Ergyfel extended his arm and pushed Dhwen off the wall. Billy exploded from the barrel as the old man plunged downward. There came the sound of tearing cloth and breaking timber as Ergyfel was dragged over the edge by his victim.

Billy stood frozen as the rain streaked down his face. He never imagined that his plan could go so wrong. It never occurred to him that someone might be killed. His knees buckled, and he fell to the ground and vomited.

A sound abruptly entered Billy's consciousness—someone grunting heavily – struggling. Impulsively, he ran to the edge of the broken wall. "Dhwen!" Billy shouted.

Billy's stomach knotted as he looked over the edge. Far below, on the ground, lay the broken body of Dhwen. One of Ergyfel's troghouls had already found the body and was shaking it like a rag. Ergyfel clung for his life to a piece of shattered scaffolding, just a few feet below.

The magister looked up at the edge and saw Billy. "You! Here to finish the job, faerie?"

"I'm no faerie."

"What does it matter now, faerie? I'm at your mercy. Exact your revenge and be done with it!"

The rickety scaffolding shook, and Ergyfel's grip started to slip. Billy's heart and mind raced. If he didn't help the magister, he would most surely fall to his death, but if he did help him …

Ergyfel is a murderer. He killed Dhwen, he's trying to kill the king, and for all I know, he might have killed the queen!

Billy looked again at Dhwen's body. Truly he was as responsible for the physician's death as the magister, or at least he felt like he was. If he let Ergyfel fall, he would be responsible for yet another death. No matter what Ergyfel had done, Billy didn't like the way that felt.

Billy quickly dug through the construction materials and found a rope. He tied one end around a crenel then ran back to the ledge.

"Here!" Billy tossed the rope to Ergyfel.

The magister eyed the rope suspiciously but did not move to catch it. It swung back to the wall below Billy.

"Take it!" Billy insisted. He swung the rope back to the First Counselor. "Take it and I'll pull you up."

"Why should I trust you, faerie?"

"Why do you say I'm a faerie? Is it the troghouls?"

"Among other things."

"Take the rope! I'll help you."

"Why should I believe you?"

Billy looked directly into the magister's black eyes. "Because you must."

Lightning flashed in the outer ward, and the scaffolding groaned ominously. The thin board Ergyfel held on to started to split under the load of his weight.

"Now!" Billy shouted.

Ergyfel released one hand and caught the rope just as the board snapped. He fell five feet before the rope became taut and swung him into the wall. The impact knocked the wind from Ergyfel's lungs, but he managed to keep hold of the rope.

Billy strained to pull the king's cousin up the wall. His back and arms ached as Ergyfel neared the top. The magister weakly reached for the ledge and Billy stretched down to help him.

Billy's arm suddenly tingled and, as he touched Ergyfel's hand, there was a blinding flash of light and the stench of burned flesh. The magister cried out in pain.

For an instant, all Billy could see was bright, stark whiteness. The brightness faded, and he found himself gazing at the serene beauty of the queen's garden.

An angry shout from the far side of the pond shattered the calm. Billy saw that the very same argument he had witnessed before was in progress. The queen's form and that of her adversary were still hazy, but Billy detected another figure, clearly standing behind the murderer. Billy focused on this figure and was drawn toward it.

He found a thin young man, little more than a boy, vaguely familiar, with an impudent, spoiled sneer. The youth silently held up a fine-boned hand and pointed a long finger in the direction of the queen. He clenched his fist, and the queen's attacker struck her down. Billy watched in horror as the youth raised his other hand, and the man put his hands around the queen's throat. The young man thrust out his hands, and like a puppet, the murderer throttled his victim. Billy wanted desperately to stop the killer but could do nothing to affect him.

When the queen's body dangled limply, the young man's lips curled into a weak, snakelike smile, and he dropped his hands. He wiped the sweat from his brow and slowly crossed to the murderer who knelt, holding his lifeless victim. He placed a hand on the assassin's shoulder, and the queen's body dropped into the pond.

A blinding light overpowered Billy's vision again. When his sight cleared, he found himself lying in a puddle, staring at dark clouds. Cold rain splashed on to his face, and he sat up, blinking the water from his eyes. He wasn't sure how long the vision had lasted, but Billy felt the lapse in his consciousness had only been a few seconds.

As Billy tried to get reoriented, the magister's thin hands slipped over the edge and clasped the broken wall. An ugly burn ran across the back of one hand, and a trickle of blood oozed from the blisters as Ergyfel used every ounce of his energy to pull himself onto the wall. He heaved his upper body onto the walkway, glaring at Billy with murderous intent. He cradled his wounded hand and gritted his teeth.

"You faeries and your cursed tricks!" he spat. "You won't think it's so funny when I –" The magister's face took on an expression of complete awe.

"The ring!" Ergyfel shouted. "You have the ring!"

Billy looked down and saw his ring glowing with an eerie blue light. He experienced a tingling in his hand as the light faded, and the ring took on its usual metallic sheen.

"So that's how Hugh defeated my dragon."

"What?"

Ergyfel stood over Billy. "Give me the ring!"

Billy scrambled to his feet and backed away. "No!"

"Give me the ring," Ergyfel repeated in a less demanding tone.

"No. It's mine!"

Ergyfel raised an eyebrow and examined his damaged hand. He sneered at Billy and then suddenly whistled. Ergyfel motioned with his fingers, and Billy realized that he was signaling to someone behind him.

Billy spun and saw two troghouls crudely loping atop the wall. His heart skipped a beat as they grinned their ugly toothy smiles at him and licked rain from their scabby lips.

"Give the ring to me, or shall I have them relieve you of it?"

Ergyfel was to Billy's left, two hungry troghouls to his right, and behind him the broken wall. Billy broke for the gap in the wall. He grabbed the rope and flung himself over the edge.

"Blast!" Ergyfel dashed to look down on his prey.

Billy quickly scrambled down the rope, but there was nowhere to go. Dhwen and Ergyfel had nearly destroyed the scaffolding, and the rope wasn't long enough to reach anything safe.

Now what? That was really stupid!

Billy looked up and saw the magister and his loathsome pets staring down at him. The King's First Counselor pulled out his dagger and tauntingly touched its edge to the rope.

"Let us cut to the chase, Billy."

"No, don't! Please!"

The magister held up his blade. "I'll ask you only one more time, you pathetic little freak. Give me the ring."

"Why?"

"Because I want it!"

"But it's mine!"

"You lie." Ergyfel cut one of three cords in Billy's rope.

Billy felt the rope stretch and nearly lost control of his bodily functions. He searched for a place to grab hold of, or a soft spot to land. Below him, the first troghoul patiently sat atop the dead physician, smiling and coaxing him down with a long, black-clawed finger.

"Just out of curiosity, little jester; where did you get it?"

Billy returned his attention to his interrogator. "It belonged to my mother."

"Your mother?" Ergyfel cut the second cord.

Billy screamed, and at that moment Ergyfel's face lost its sneer. His eyes shifted from side to side, and his lips slowly formed a crooked smile—first one side of his mouth and then the other. The magister threw back his head and crowed at the sky. When his face came back down, he smiled diabolically at Billy.

"So, boy, you still live! But don't worry. When you fall to your death, I'll be sure to take the ring from your bloody finger."

A stroke of lightning lit up the First Counselor's face, and Billy felt as if he had been struck through the heart. The spoiled, arrogant countenance of the young man who had orchestrated the queen's murder stared back at him.

"You killed the queen," Billy said numbly.

"And now you shall finally join her." Ergyfel cut into the rope.

Billy cried out and wildly waved his arms as the last cord of his lifeline snapped. He crashed through one board and then another, before a scaffolding cross-member caught under his arm. Despite the sharp pain this caused his ribs, Billy managed to hold on to the beam.

"Blast!" Ergyfel shouted from above. "Confound you! Will you not die?"

Billy glanced over his shoulder at the magister, then back to the troghoul still waiting below. For the mean time he was safe—if he could just hold on until help arrived.

"Go after him!" Ergyfel shouted.

Billy twisted around and watched as the magister dragged one of his offensive watchdogs to the edge of the wall and kicked it. The beast tried to remain where it was, but its balance was too far forward and its footing too slippery. The monster, realizing its predicament, made the best of it and leapt towards Billy.

Down the troghoul came, with teeth bared and claws spread. Billy gripped the beam with his legs and closed his eyes, preparing to meet with his end. A moment later, Billy felt a sharp pain in his arm and the entire scaffolding set in motion. The remaining structure swayed with a creak and a groan.

Billy opened his eyes and found himself inches away from the troghoul. One claw of the miscreant pierced his arm while all its remaining weapons held firmly to the beam. The monster tilted its ugly face to the side and presented a full spread of large, yellow fangs. Even in the rain, the stench from its mouth was overwhelming. It snickered at him and impishly withdrew its claw from his flesh. Billy felt the pain stiffening his arm, sapping his strength. The beast sniffed its bloody claw, and its eyes grew large. Quickly, it licked Billy's blood from its extremity, closing its eyes with an expression of ecstasy. Its breathing quickened and grew deeper, and Billy carefully inched away.

"What's taking you so long?" Ergyfel shouted. "Just kill him!"

The troghoul lifted up its face into the rain and let loose a horrible, bloody howl, which excited the others into yapping, frenzied howls. Billy's blood ran cold. Much too soon for Billy, the beast returned its gaze to him. Its eyes swelled with lusty hunger, and its body shook with pent-up, berserk energy.

All at once, the troghoul lunged at Billy. The jarring movement tore free the beam, which instantly batted the beast from the air. Billy clamped on to the timber with all his might and was soon swinging upside down as it danced and dangled from its shaky upright.

Below Billy hung the gory body of his would-be killer, its spine clearly shattered by a splintered spar that impaled it through the chest. Billy clenched his eyes tightly against the image of twisted, twitching flesh.

"Ho there!" someone shouted from a distance.

Billy opened his eyes. Ergyfel was squinting down the length of the wall towards the donjon.

"Curse and confound you!" the magister raged through clenched teeth. He gave Billy a dark look so filled with bloody intent that Billy's fear of falling completely evaporated. "You might yet survive this night, brat, but our dear Kathryn will not be so lucky!" With a snap of his cloak, the dark sorcerer turned and vanished into the darkness.

"Ho there!" The voice was now closer. "Stop!"

"Down here!" Billy yelled. The blood rushing to his head made shouting extremely painful.

The troghoul on the wall crouched low and bared its teeth. Billy could hear footsteps from above and the creature growling, then the ring of metal sliding across metal. Instantly the beast leapt from Billy's view. There came a hollow thump and the skitter of loose rocks skipping across the stone wall. The creature let out a near-human cry, which abruptly sputtered to a gurgle, then was silent. The only sound Billy could hear was the applause of the rain.

Billy called out. "I'm down here! I'm down here."

There was no answer, and then Billy heard the creak of the scaffolding as it shifted further from the wall. He remembered the remaining troghoul beneath him and looked down. With glittering eyes, the beast stared up at him. It growled and then slipped away into the shadows.

"William!" a voice shouted from above.

Billy looked up and saw Gaelyn standing at the breach in the wall, his bloodied dagger in hand. Hastily, the prince scanned the wall and then ducked out of view.

"Come back!" Billy could feel himself growing weaker. His head pounded painfully with each beat of his heart, but he didn't dare let go of the beam. Billy tapped his deepest reserves as his weakness continued to grow. He was losing his grip, and Gaelyn still had not returned.

I have to warn Kathryn.

Billy started to cry. "Come back, Gaelyn," he muttered. "Please, come back."

At that moment a rope dropped next to Billy. Forthwith, the prince shinnied down it. As he arrived next to Billy, the timbers groaned loudly. Gaelyn snagged Billy's belt with a free hand, and the scaffolding collapsed with an enormous crash.

Billy clung to the prince's muscular leg, his energy all but gone. His mind and hands could no longer function. He had to wrap his arms and legs around his savior to keep from falling.

Slowly, Prince Gaelyn pulled himself and Billy back onto the wall. The downpour worsened, but they didn't care. They collapsed on the wet stones and stared at each other through the drops, too tired to say anything.

Eventually, the prince caught his breath. "What on earth happened here, William?"

Billy numbly answered. "You wouldn't believe me if I told you."

He scanned the body of the troghoul a few feet away. The prince had made quick work of the beast with a single wound to the chest. Its crumpled form reminded Billy of the other troghoul, and of Dhwen. Billy dragged himself to the gap in the wall and looked down. The lifeless body of the old man still lay in an awkward heap at the foot of the wall. Billy closed his eyes, wishing he could forget; wishing he could take it all back.

How foolish I've been. Foolish and arrogant!

Billy's mind conjured up a vision of the dead physician's family, people he had never met but had managed to harm just the same. Billy hung his head and wept.

CHAPTER TWENTY

Hullabaloo

"Kathryn!" Billy shouted, finally coming to his senses.
"Kathryn?" Gaelyn repeated.

Billy leapt to his feet and grabbed Gaelyn by the arm. "We've got to stop him!" He then pulled the noble to his feet.

"Who? What?"

"He's gonna kill her!" Billy shouted and ran towards the donjon. Gaelyn gave chase, following Billy the length of the wall. "Who's going to kill whom?" he asked between breaths.

Billy never slowed down as he descended the steps and crossed the vacant inner ward. Prince Gaelyn, despite his athletic physique and superior length of stride, could hardly keep up with him.

"Guards! Guards!" Billy shouted.

As they entered the donjon, Billy felt a strange sensation. He slowed to a stop and scanned the entry hall.

Gaelyn came up behind him. "What is it? What's going on?"

Billy glanced about nervously. "The guards!"

Gaelyn cast his eye about the entry hall. As usual, there was a guard standing watch at each corner. He didn't see any reason for concern.

Billy grabbed the guard at the entrance and shook him. The man leaned and then slumped forward. A moment later, his helmet and spear smacked the floor. Billy stepped back as the guard's body came crashing down at his feet.

Gaelyn looked to the other guards for a reaction, but they didn't move. "What the devil?"

Billy poked the downed guard, who smiled, mumbled, and rolled into a fetal position. When Billy's kick had no reaction, he said, "He's asleep!"

Gaelyn took the guard nearest the stairway by the shoulders and shook him. "Wake up, man!"

The guard smiled and oozed into the prince's arms. Gaelyn caught him and held him up against the wall.

Billy started up the stairs. "Hurry!"

The prince grabbed Billy by the wrist and spun him around. "Tell me what the devil is happening here!"

Billy broke free from his grip and ran up the stairs. "It's Ergyfel! He's trying to kill Kathryn!"

Prince Gaelyn threw the guard to the floor and charged up the steps. He passed Billy before they reached the top and ran through the empty hallways toward the royal chambers.

"Alarm!" Gaelyn shouted. "Alarm!"

Billy and the prince raced on and reached the royal wing without seeing a single guard, servant, or guest. Billy became unbearably frightened as they passed his room and saw the door to the newlywed's chamber ajar.

Prince Gaelyn never lost stride as he drew his dagger and slammed into the door. The oak panel exploded away from him with a crash, and he continued into the central chamber. Billy entered the room on the prince's tail.

A dark figure crouched in the dimly lit archway of the balcony. It was a slender man dressed entirely in black, his face hidden behind a veil. He held a long curved blade in his hand and between his feet laid a body. By the color of her hair and the beautiful dress, Billy knew it was Princess Kathryn.

"NO!" Billy forgot himself and ran forward.

THE JESTER | 65

Gaelyn screamed, "Kathryn!" and charged.

The assassin readied himself for the prince's attack.

Suddenly, Billy tripped and smacked his jaw on the floor. He blinked, fighting to remain conscious. He looked beside him and saw Gwyn, the princess' maid, her pale face staring vacantly from a dark pool of blood. Billy rolled away quickly and came face to face with Arlyn, who was also dead. Billy sprang to his feet and away from the corpses.

Steel clashed on steel as the prince and the murderer engaged in combat. Gaelyn's opponent thrust and chopped at him with his long blade. Each time, Gaelyn just managed to parry the weapon away with his dagger. It appeared to Billy that Gaelyn was outclassed, if only because of the killer's superior reach. Unless help came soon, Gaelyn would lose the fight.

"Guards! Alarm!" Billy shouted as he looked for an opening to help the prince.

The assassin missed Gaelyn again, and the prince closed on him. Before the murderer could bring his sword down, Prince Gaelyn grabbed his wrist and countered with a dagger thrust. The man dodged the attack with the skill of a dancer and caught the prince's weapon hand.

As the combatants wrestled, Billy advanced to Princess Kathryn. "Guards!" he shouted as he arrived by her side.

Billy knelt beside his princess, who lay facedown on the floor. He scooped one hand under her and used the other to cradle her head. He had to use his own weight to turn her over but slipped on the slick stone floor and wound up sitting with the princess in his lap. Billy's heart froze when he saw her face, with mouth and eyes open wide in astonishment. Her blood flowed warm onto him like fresh milk. He put his hands over the wounds, trying to staunch the flow, but there was nothing he could do. Kathryn was dead.

Billy's entire being shook with outrage, and he scooted away from the princess. "Murderer!" he shouted at the dark man and charged him.

Prince Gaelyn and the killer were still locked together when Billy tackled the assassin. Billy's momentum carried the three of them out onto the balcony. The prince tripped at the doorway, and they all fell.

The murderer's sword arm was trapped under Prince Gaelyn as they splashed down on the wet balcony. The prince struck at his opponent's heart with his dagger, just inches from Billy's eyes. The killer deftly blocked the deadly blow with his arm but was not so lucky when the prince quickly drew the weapon towards his face. The prince's blade slashed down the length of the assassin's forearm and crossed his palm.

"Ayeee!" the killer exclaimed. He dropped his sword and rolled away.

Prince Gaelyn lunged again at his retreating enemy, but only managed to cut open the back of his shirt. In the blink of an eye, the murderer leapt to his feet and faced the still prone prince with a thin black knife in his hand.

Billy stared at the weapon that seemed to appear magically in the assassin's grip. A single raindrop landed on the blade and hung there as if stuck.

"Poison!" Billy muttered.

Instantly the killer dove at Gaelyn. The prince managed to get his feet and hands out to catch his assailant and fling him over his head to the opposite side of the balcony. The man landed on a chair and shattered it, but again rolled into a crouched fighting stance. Billy, now on his feet, marveled at the assassin's agility.

Quickly, the killer turned the knife in his hand so that the blade was under and parallel to his wrist. Prince Gaelyn grabbed the assassin's sword and kicked up to a fighting stance. The murderer's eyes flashed an expression of surprise and then narrowed as he gazed down the length of his own sword in the hand of his enemy.

The assassin changed his stance, holding his left hand out in front of him. Billy could see that the wound on his palm cut deep. What remained of the killer's sleeve was soaked in blood. The hand wielding the poisoned weapon, he held low.

The prince charged into the murderer, swinging the long curved blade as well as his own dagger. The first swings forced the assassin back. Then suddenly he thrust at the prince—his attack timed perfectly to slip between Gaelyn's whirling blades. Gaelyn jumped back, narrowly avoiding the dark blade, but as the killer drew the knife back in, it kissed the prince's cheek.

"Blast!" Gaelyn exclaimed.

The prince redoubled his attack, and his opponent retreated by leaping on to the balustrade. Gaelyn slashed at the killer's legs, but then his swings slowed abruptly. He was weakening fast. Again and again the man in black leapt away from the sword, like a child jumping rope. Gaelyn stumbled and shook his head. The assassin straightened confidently.

Without warning, Gaelyn slashed out and up. The blade bit into the already injured hand, turning the long cut into a cross in the middle of his palm. The man cried out in pain, and Gaelyn advanced to finish him.

As Gaelyn thrust forward, to drive the murderer over the edge, the man suddenly flipped over the prince's head and landed behind him on the balcony. Gaelyn slammed into the balustrade. Instantly, the assassin drove his weapon into Gaelyn's unprotected back.

Gaelyn spun around to face the killer. He dragged one foot forward, staring the man in the eyes. A thin strand of blood drooled from his mouth, and he dropped to his knees. His weapons dangled harmlessly in his hands and then fell from his grip. His eyes meandered for a moment before focusing on Billy. "Run for your li—" he whispered then fell facedown on the wet balcony.

Billy turned and ran for the door. "Guards!" he screamed. "Alarm!" Before he could make another sound, he felt a sharp pain in the back of his head, and he slipped into unconsciousness.

* * *

Billy opened his eyes. Darkness was all around him. The floor he lay on was hard and cold. His head felt like a well-used anvil. The smell of wet, moldy straw and filth filled his nose. He blinked and held his hand up before his face, but still all he could see was the darkest black.

At that moment he became aware of something heavy around his wrist that cut into his flesh. Billy fumbled in the darkness and found that his wrists, waist, and ankles were all chained together. Billy also found that if he straightened his legs, his hands were pulled to his waist. Then he tried to stand but bumped his head on the ceiling of his little cell.

"Ow!" he exclaimed as the blow intensified his headache. "Stupid roof is too low!"

"You're lucky you can stand," stated a low, raspy voice from the darkness.

Billy spun around to face the voice but only managed to become tangled in his chains and have the wind knocked out of him as he was thrown to the floor.

"Not wise," the voice croaked.

Billy coughed as he strained to catch his breath. After a moment, his breath returned, and he sat up. Billy squinted, trying to somehow pierce the inky darkness. Finally he gave up and asked, "Who are you?"

"I? … I? … I'm nobody."

"Where am I?"

"Nowhere."

"No!" Billy insisted. "Where am I?"

"The last place you ever wanted to be."

"Which is?"

"Hell."

"Hell?"

"Aye. The darkest, deepest pit in that infernal kingdom."

"Am I dead?" Billy asked most earnestly.

"I hope not!" his cellmate answered. "The dead are terribly boring – just lie there, rotting away, smelling up the place. But with my luck, you probably are."

"I was in Castle Orgulous—"

"And you still are."

"But I thought ya said … Where exactly are we?"

"This is an oubliette," Billy's companion stated.

"A what?"

"An oubliette!" The stranger sounded perturbed. "It's where they put you if they want to forget you—or was it if they want you to forget them? I can't remember anymore."

"I'm Billy."

Billy waited for his new acquaintance to introduce himself, but silence was his only answer.

"I'm Billy, the king's musician. And you are …?"

"Didn't I tell you already? I'm nobody."

"Everybody's somebody."

"Not me. I'm nobody, and if you're smart, you'll be nobody too."

"Well … nobody … Nobody who?"

"Nobody to be trifled with, boy!" the man hissed.

Billy suddenly felt menace behind the man's words. Without warning, he felt the man's presence nearby and imagined hands around his throat.

"I didn't get here by playing the wrong note, musician!"

The man fell silent and Billy moved away from him until he came to a wall. For a moment, Billy thought he could see someone sitting across from him, but then the image dissolved, and he decided it was only his imagination. The man still said nothing, and so Billy waited.

At last, Billy's patience ran out, and he asked, "Can ya ever see anything in this darkness?"

"No," the man answered, his voice croaking calmly. "Not unless they were to let you out. And then the Dark One brings light to stab your eyes like fire!"

"How long have you been in here?" Billy asked.

"Years, decades … What does it matter in an eternity?"

"What did ya do to be put here?"

"My crimes are so vile that you would burn in Hell just to hear them, boy! I am a beast, a monster, a fouler, more loathsome criminal than you could ever imagine!"

They fell silent again. Billy was afraid to say anything. His cellmate was obviously a raving lunatic, and by his own admission a murderer or worse, if there was something worse.

When Billy thought he might never hear it again, the faceless voice of his cellmate spoke, nearly scaring him out of his skin.

"Why are you here, boy?"

Billy calmed himself down and thought about the question. He couldn't think of anything that would have him thrown into the dungeon. The last thing he remembered was ...

"The prince." Billy whispered. His head was filled with images of Gaelyn's and Kathryn's death.

"What?"

"I don't know," Billy said.

"Don't know what?"

"I don't know why I'm here."

"Me neither."

"What?"

"I don't know why I'm here either."

"But-but-but your crimes—" stammered Billy.

"What crimes?"

"You said you had committed foul, monstrous deeds!"

"I did? Oh yes, I did."

"Well ...?"

"Well, I couldn't remember ... so I made it up."

"Made it up?"

"I must have done somethin' to be here. I though it sounded pretty good, didn't you?"

"Made it up?"

"Shhhh! Someone's comin'."

"I didn't hear anything."

"Shhhh!"

Billy listened carefully and heard keys rattling in a faraway lock, then the creak of a door followed by footsteps. Next he heard three muffled voices. Ergyfel's was among them.

"I just don't understand why you're here, Magister."

"I wish to see the prisoner," Ergyfel said. "That is all you need to know. Is he awake yet, jailer?"

"Last time I checked, he was still out," the third man answered.

"Open it," Ergyfel commanded. "I wish to see him."

There was another rattle as someone fiddled with a latch above. A small hatch opened in the ceiling, and a shaft of light struck Billy in the eyes. It was only the light of torches, but to Billy it was as painful as staring into the sun.

Billy tuned away from the light. By squinting, his eyes were able to make out a dirty, wretched, emaciated man with grey scraggly hair and a beard, cowering in the corner. A shadow blotted out most of the light, and Billy looked to the hatch. A man stood over the small hole, looking down at him. All Billy could see was his silhouette.

"Leave us," Ergyfel said.

"What, milord?"

"You're half blind now. Are you half deaf as well? I said, leave us, before I take your other eye!"

Billy heard the two men walk away. Ergyfel waited until they had closed the distant door before he spoke.

"How do you like your new accommodations, elf?"

"Why am I here, Ergyfel?"

"And what of your new roommate, eh? We nearly forgot he was down there. Now if we could only remember what he's done ... Oh well, I guess he'll just have to stay there until *he* remembers." Ergyfel laughed and stomped the floor. "You hear that, old man?"

Billy's cellmate whimpered and curled up tighter to the wall.

Billy's pity turned to anger. "Why am I here?"

"Because I wish it."

"How long are you going to keep me here?"

Ergyfel answered as if he were discussing where to hang a tapestry. "Until I can decide what to do with you."

"Do with me?"

"It's not often I have to decide the fate of an assassin."

"Assassin? But I tried to stop it! You're the one—"

"Oh yes, I can see you now, pleading your case before the king. 'I'm innocent, Your Majesty. I tried to stop the killer, Your Majesty. I did!'" Ergyfel laughed. "'It was Ergyfel, your First Counselor, your cousin, the only one you'll listen to …' You'd be very convincing, I'm sure."

"I'll tell him everything about you!"

"Save your breath. Even if you were allowed to speak, it would not matter. I've planned this far too well, and since the coronation fell through … well, I've had time to tidy up. You fit into my plans like a snail in its shell. No one will believe you didn't do it—not in the face of the considerable evidence I've gathered against you."

"You mean evidence you created!"

Ergyfel chuckled. "Do you know the punishment for assassins? No? Shall I give you a hint?" He leaned forward and whispered through the tiny hatch. "By the time they're done with you, Billy, the biggest piece anyone will find won't fill a bucket! That is what waits for you, unless—"

"Unless what?" Billy asked

"Unless you give me the ring."

"My ring?"

"Yes."

"But I can't."

"Then as I stated before," Ergyfel said, examining his fingernails, "I will just have to pry it from your dead little finger."

"But I—"

"But nothing," Ergyfel said. "I have all the evidence I need to have you executed now!"

Ergyfel paused, and Billy heard him pacing overhead. He looked up and saw the magister holding the hand that the ring had burned.

Ergyfel continued. "However, since I'd much rather have the ring sooner than later, I'm giving you a chance to get out of this alive."

"How do I know you'll keep your word?"

Ergyfel laughed. "Now it is *you*, who must trust *me*. Look, my little friend, give me the ring, and I'll say you were just in the wrong place at the wrong time. The king will believe me. Kathryn and Gaelyn are already dead. There isn't anything you can do or say that will bring them back, and no one—no one—will believe a story that implicates me. Why not just give it up and live with it? Live. Choose my way, and we both win. You get your life, and I get the ring."

"And the kingdom."

"Well," the magister said, "my cousin's not dead yet."

"What's so important about this old ring?"

"I'm beginning to lose my patience, little man."

"What's so important?"

"Nothing that would interest you." Ergyfel's tone grew angry. "Isn't it enough that I want it?"

"But what can it do for you?"

"The question is: what can it do for *you*?"

"Hunh?"

"Shall I tell you, my diminutive friend?" Ergyfel crouched close to the small opening. He whispered as he had done before. "That ring contains the power of life and death. It can save your life."

"How?"

Ergyfel became deadly serious. "Give it to me and you live. Keep it and you die. It's that simple."

Billy rolled Ergyfel's offer over in his mind. *My life for the ring? But there's more at stake than just me, or an old ring. What's he up to?*

"Well ...?" Ergyfel said impatiently.

"I'm thinking!"

"You're dying."

Ergyfel seemed unstoppable, and if he sat on the throne, the kingdom would be ruined. Billy contemplated all the people whose lives would be destroyed if this ever came to pass. He didn't understand it, but he knew his mother's ring was somehow a part of it. He also believed that Ergyfel would kill him in the end, no matter what he did.

Billy looked up at Ergyfel. "No."

"Fool!" The magister straightened. "You only delay the inevitable."

Ergyfel kicked the hatch closed, and Billy heard the bolt find its home. There was a chilly finality in the way it latched.

"You'll wish you had listened to me, elf."

Billy felt a surge of anger. "I'll get you Ergyfel! I promise!"

Billy listened as the magister's footsteps faded away. He fell to the floor—all the energy in his body drained away. He felt so hopeless.

"You speak in such tones to the Dark One?"

Billy looked in the direction of his invisible friend. "Ergyfel?"

"The Evil One!" the man cried.

"He's evil all right, but he is not the devil."

"He speaks to me sometimes in my dreams. He takes away the light. He frightens me."

"He frightens me too," Billy said half to himself.

Billy wished his father would come and take him home to his cozy, soft bed. He lay down and cried himself to sleep.

Billy was roused by a voice that whispered his name. "Father?" he said, squinting in the light. "What is it, Father?"

"It's not your father, Billy."

"What?"

"It's me, Gryff."

"Gryff?"

Billy had been dreaming of his father and the home he had left behind in the Valley of the Yew. As he regained his senses, the awful reality of his current predicament smacked him in the face. "Gryff?" he exclaimed. "What are you doin' here?"

"I come to bring ya some food, but that's not all. I brung ya some parchment and a quill."

"What?"

"To write a letter to Sir Hugh or Lady Myrredith. Surely they will come if ya tell them what's happened."

"But how will I get it to them?"

"Let me worry about that," Gryff answered. "Now quickly, lad. I haven't much time."

Billy quickly penned a note to Lady Myrredith, under the shaft of light from the small hatch. He then read it to Gryff.

"Myrredith, I am in terrible trouble. Ergyfel has murdered Princess Kathryn and Prince Gaelyn. I tried to stop it, but was too late. Ergyfel has me locked in the dungeon. Please come quickly, Ergyfel has also poisoned King William and I don't know how to save him. I know that if you and Sir Hugh come, you can save me and the king. Signed Billy."

Gryff took the letter. "Good. I'll see that this gets into the right hands. Now I must go."

"Thank you, Gryff." Billy took Gryff's hand.

"It's nothin'. It'll be fine, lad. You'll see."

"Luck," Billy said.

"And to you," Gryff offered. Then he closed the hatch and left.

Billy waited in the darkness. Neither he nor his new companion had the mind to converse. He waited and slept, waited and slept, on and on, until he had no idea of what time or even what day it was. Occasionally food came through the little hatch, but nary a word from any who were outside.

Billy awoke to the sounds of someone coming. Not the sound of one or two, in soft shoes, as when food was brought, but the heavy tramping of many wearing heavy boots. It grew louder until they were directly on top of the cell. Billy heard the sound of chains being pulled through a pulley, and suddenly a crack of light appeared in a large square pattern over his head. Slowly the crack expanded, becoming too bright for Billy to gaze upon. He closed his eyes and waited. Without warning, two men reached down into the little cell and grabbed Billy under his arms.

"Wha—"

A large rough hand punched Billy in the mouth.

"Gag him," the man ordered, and a dirty rag was thrust into Billy's mouth and tied around his head. "The magister don't want him charmin' nobody with his evil faerie magic."

Billy squinted until his eyes became more accustomed to the light. There were eight men in a small, round chamber. All but one was wearing armor and weapons. He had a large key ring in his hand and a scar that ran over one eye, closing it up. Two of the armored men lowered the heavy cover back onto the pit, in the center of the floor. Meanwhile, two others ran a spear through Billy's chains and picked him up like hunters carrying a deer carcass. The men carried Billy from the room, down the long hallway, and through the door, which Billy had only heard before.

They went up and up, ascending one set of steps after the other. Finally, they came to a large platform with an iron door. As the jailer opened the door, bright light flooded in, blinding Billy completely. Now Billy knew what his cellmate had meant by the stabbing light.

It was some time before Billy could bring himself to open even one eyelid a crack. However, soon after he had accomplished this, his eyes were able to see without the burning pain. He knew that he was in one of the corridors of Castle Orgulous, *but where?* The guards marched on in silence. Billy so much wanted to ask where they were taking him. Then his question was answered.

The small squad carrying Billy came to a door with two guards. The man leading the squad ordered the guards to open the door, and they entered. As they cleared the doorway, Billy saw the ceiling of the king's great hall. He also heard the sound of Ergyfel's voice.

"Ah, here is the miscreant now," Ergyfel said.

Suddenly, the screams and jeers of hundreds of angry people accosted Billy's ears. He looked to either side and saw a huge crowd of lords and commoners behind a solid row of guardsmen. All of them pointed at him and yelled foul, horrible names. Some had to be restrained by the guards as they tried to cross the picket line. Their eyes were wild and full of hate.

Billy saw faces that he knew but could hardly recognize them. *Are these the same people who cheered me only a few days ago?*

The guards dropped Billy on the floor and formed a semicircle behind him. In front of Billy, down each side of the hall, were the majority of the court's lords and ladies, again behind a curtain of guards. The king sat at the end of the hall, sadly stroking his beard and staring at Billy. Hovering nearby, like a carrion bird, was the dark figure of the King's First Counselor. His mouth was frowning, but Billy could see him laughing behind his cold ebony eyes.

Ergyfel held up his hands for the court to be silent. Billy noticed a bandage around the First Counselor's hand where the ring had burned him. The crowd continued to shout and jeer.

"Silence!" the magister shouted angrily. His voice boomed over the din and reverberated even after the mob quieted. He then pointed a long, bony finger at Billy. "Stand!"

Billy got to his feet and faced Ergyfel.

"Your Majesty," the King's First Counselor said, "what is thy bidding?"

Billy watched while King William stared blankly at the floor. *What could he be thinking?*

"I believe," the king said weakly, "I believe we should let the prisoner and this assembly hear your evidence before I pass judgment."

"The evidence is quite overwhelming, Your Majesty," Ergyfel stated.

"It is in accordance with my laws. Are you not up to it, cousin?"

"No, Your Majesty. I ... I only worry about your health."

"Do not worry for me, cousin," the king said. "As you know, I have a fondness for the boy. It will take some effort on your part, to convince me that he is the villain we seek."

"As Your Majesty wishes."

The magister turned and signaled to a guardsmen near the end of the great hall. The man came forward, carrying a box that he placed at the feet of the King's First Counselor. Ergyfel dismissed the man and reached into the box. He pulled out the knife that Billy had seen the assassin use.

"Your Majesty," Ergyfel started, "this knife is the weapon used to slay our dear cousin, Princess Kathryn—"

A murmur rose from the crowd.

"And ..." Ergyfel raised his voice over the hubbub. "And her beloved husband Prince Gaelyn, whom we had all come to love and respect."

"Here, here!" came several cheers from the crowd.

Ergyfel held up his hand for silence. When the room was quiet, he continued. "Its blade is poisoned."

The crowd grumbled again.

"My fellow countrymen, please!" Ergyfel pleaded. "I have discovered a great deal of disturbing evidence, and I know how terribly you want justice, but please try to control yourselves."

The mob quieted.

"Thank you. To continue ..." Ergyfel paced around the box, his eyes on the floor. "When the murders were discovered, the prisoner's clothing was drenched in blood, and I had the guards search his room. What they found ..." The king's counselor reached into the box again. "was this!"

The magister held up a second knife. It was the twin to the first.

"They are identical, Your Majesty. A matched set, down to the poison!"

Again the crowd had to be put down. They all shouted at Billy and demanded his death. Finally the king held up his hand to quiet the mob.

"Is this all the evidence, Ergyfel?" the king asked.

"No, Your Majesty. As you know, I have warned you all about the faerie folk and the evil threat they pose to us."

"Yes, yes." King William waved his hand is if shooing at a fly. "But what does that have to do with this? Surely you are not implying that William here is a faerie!"

The king laughed, and the crowd followed his example. Billy could see Ergyfel's ears turn red, and the muscles in his jaw tighten.

"Your Majesty!" Ergyfel cried over the noisy mob. "Your Majesty, I'm afraid that you have gotten ahead of me. Please allow me to finish. The apothecary has analyzed the poison on these blades. He tells me it is derived from birch, bluebells, and toadstools, a deadly concoction known as faerie venom."

Ergyfel's audience was now very quiet. Only Billy was close enough to see the satisfaction on his face. He was performing now.

"I fail to see the connection," the king said.

"I think you will in just a moment, Sire. I would like you to hear something that may surprise and even shock you." The magister then turned to the crowd and waved for someone to come forward.

There was a commotion as somebody pushed their way to the front of the crowd. Billy watched with great curiosity. At last a well-rounded friar appeared. Billy recognized him as the same priest he had chased through the orchard in Dyven. The guards let him through, into the center of the hall. He bowed to the king and then faced the magister.

Ergyfel addressed the fat priest. "Good friar, could you please tell us where you come from?"

The humble priest answered. "I am Brother Angal. My home is in Dyven, in the abbey there. I came here to witness the wedding and coronation of the late princess. The abbot wished me to record these events for posterity. Alas, I was delayed and missed the wedding."

"Yes, and tell me, friar, have you ever seen the prisoner before?"

"Oh yes!" The priest crossed himself. He was sweating profusely.

"Good friar, you seem a bit frightened."

"As would be any God-fearing man who had seen what I have."

"Please, tell us what you saw."

"Well," the friar said, "I was out in our orchard, collecting some apples, when I spied a hare. I thought that perhaps the good Lord had sent this fine hare to feed my brothers and me. I couldn't have been more wrong."

"Please explain, friar."

"When I chased the hare into an older part of the orchard—a place where pagans once buried their dead—it changed into a boy. It changed into him!" The priest pointed at Billy.

The crowd gasped.

Ergyfel stepped forward. "You mean to tell us, that the hare became this boy?"

"Aye." The priest crossed himself again. "I saw the devil-sent demon transform before my very eyes."

Billy wanted to scream out that the priest was a liar as a multitude of cries erupted from the crowd. He wanted to remove his gag and proclaim to the whole world that Ergyfel had manipulated the whole thing and that Ergyfel was the guilty one. Billy tried to reach his gag but couldn't raise his hands above his waist. Quickly he squatted and thrust up with his hands to reach his mouth.

Ergyfel shouted, "Stop him!" and two guardsmen grabbed Billy.

Billy struggled with the guards, and the crowd redoubled its noisy anarchy. Two more guards came to aid of their comrades with the squirming, kicking juggler.

The king rose shakily to his feet and held up his hand for quiet. Guards around the room had to resort to force to restore the peace. Finally all was still, including Billy. Every eye was on the king.

"Why not ..." the king began, before he was taken by a coughing fit. When the king had sat on his throne again and regained his breath he continued. "Why not let the boy speak for himself?"

Ergyfel rushed forward towards the king. "Your Majesty! Allowing him to speak would be inviting him to charm us all with some evil enchantment!"

"I am not convinced that the boy has any magical powers."

"But, Your Majesty, he is not a boy!"

"Then what is he?"

"A faerie assassin, sent to murder our family and overthrow the kingdom. Dhwen found this out, and was on his way to warn me. That's when the prisoner murdered him."

The crowd gasped.

The king stiffened. "Dhwen's death was not an accident?"

"I'm afraid there is little doubt of that, Your Majesty. Shortly before the feast I hosted that night, I saw your physician and the prisoner on the inter-bailey wall, directly above where his body was found. At the time, I thought little of it, but that was before this faerie murdered our cousins!"

Ergyfel raged and shook his fist at Billy. The mob followed his lead until the king spoke.

"Cousin," the king shouted. "Cousin, please!" When the rabble had quieted, he continued. "If the prisoner is truly a faerie, as you say, then why hasn't he turned himself into a bird and—"

Billy saw the magister make a tight fist, and the king succumbed to another coughing fit. Billy watched closely as he released his fist, and the king recovered.

Ergyfel pointed at Billy. "The prisoner's chains are wrought from iron, Your Majesty, and iron is a powerful agent against faerie magic. He cannot change his form while thusly bound."

King William pondered this before nodding. "Proceed."

Ergyfel tipped his head to the king. "Please, Your Majesty. Allow me to show you the most damning piece of evidence."

"Very well."

"It is a letter sent by the prisoner to the Lady of Cyndyn Hall. I intercepted it by chance, before it could leave Orgulous."

Billy thought back to the letter he had written to his patron lady. There was nothing damning in that letter. In truth it was quite the opposite. Billy watched as Ergyfel lifted a parchment from the box. It appeared to be the same letter he had written.

What could he be up to?

Ergyfel turned to Billy and showed him the bottom of the parchment. "Is this your signature?"

Billy examined it. At first glance it appeared to be his letter, and the signature at the bottom was definitely his. However, there was something odd about it. The way it laid on the page looked different from the way he remembered it, and the letters appeared smeared and fuzzy.

Ergyfel pulled the letter away from Billy's sight and grabbed hold of his chains. He pulled upwards until the manacles cut into Billy's flesh and forced him to stand on tiptoes.

"I compel you, by the iron that binds you, faerie! Now tell me, is this your signature?"

The audience was still as they waited for Billy's response. At last, he nodded his head in the affirmative.

Ergyfel released Billy. "Your Majesty, I would like for the good friar to read us this letter."

The king nodded, and Ergyfel handed the letter to the priest. The priest took a moment to look at it. His eyes became large and his skin pale. He swallowed deeply to prepare for reading the parchment.

"Myrredith, I am in terrible trouble. I has murdered the Princess Kathryn and Prince Gaelyn. Ergyfel tried to stop it, but was too late. I has also ..." The priest stopped cold, as his hands trembled.

"What is it, good friar?" Ergyfel asked.

"It's-it's-I cannot."

The king shifted in his seat. "Please, Brother Angal, read on. I command it."

The friar sighed and returned his eyes to the letter. "I has also poisoned ... King William."

A low murmur rippled through the crowd and came crashing back as a wave of outraged cries. The priest stopped again.

Ergyfel turned to his audience. "Please! Let him finish!"

The friar swallowed and wiped the sweat from his brow before continuing. "And Ergyfel don't know how to save him. And Ergyfel has me locked in the king dungeon. Please come quickly, I know that if you and Sir Hugh come, you can save me."

"Is that all?"

The friar looked at Ergyfel. "The letter is signed ... Billy."

The crowd instantly surpassed its prior level. Many people charged the guard line trying to break through to Billy. The guards held them, but they were losing ground to the rabble. Immediately, the captain of the guard ordered the detail that brought Billy to take him away.

As Billy was carried away, the perimeter guardsmen lost control, and the angry mob charged across the hall after him. The small squad with Billy passed through a low door and slammed it shut behind them. They immediately dropped Billy, barred the door, and reinforced it with their bodies.

Billy waited. The roar behind the door went on for minutes. Several times the door shook with a loud thump as it was struck from the opposite side. Billy heard the sounds of fighting. Finally the noise subsided, and the guards relaxed. They waited in the little hallway outside the great hall, listening.

"My fellow countrymen," Ergyfel said, "it is obvious we have the culprit. It is also obvious that we have the situation in hand. Because of the tragic nature of this business we are willing to be lenient this one time, but do not overtax our patience! Please return to your places and hear the judgment of the king."

Billy and the guards waited several minutes more as the assembly shuffled about the hall. It sounded like the hum from a beehive.

Several of the guards turned their attention to their prisoner. Billy looked at each of them. Their grim, sneering faces spoke volumes.

The king addressed the assembly. "My good people, the nature of this crime has left me without words. However, let me assure you that, though

it grieves me, his punishment for this act will be—and indeed, must be—
the harshest known to the law."

"And what of his conspirators?" Ergyfel demanded.

"His conspirators?"

"Why yes, Your Majesty. The letter indicates that Sir Hugh and Lady
Myrredith might well have been involved."

The crowd had to be quieted again after this statement. The guards
with Billy shook their heads.

"Not possible," one of them said. "Sir Hugh's no traitor!"

"I fail to see how they are implicated," the king stated. "Sir Hugh is our
faithful champion. As for Lady Myrredith, the lords of Cyndyn are our
distant cousins and have been loyal to us for generations."

"But the letter—!"

"Are you bringing charges, Magister?"

"Yes, Your Majesty."

"Very well," the king said, "the execution of the prisoner will take place
after such time as Sir Hugh and Lady Myrredith of Cyndyn have come
before us to answer these charges."

"No!" Ergyfel shouted.

The entire hall fell silent, except for King William, who fell into
another violent coughing fit. When the king had recovered, he spoke.
"The prisoner shall be held in our dungeon until such time as his presence
in our court is necessary—"

"But—"

"Be that to face us, or those whom you accuse, or ... to face his
execution."

Above the hubbub, Billy heard a heavily accented voice. "I beg Your
Majesty's forgiveness, but might I be allowed to speak?"

The room hushed.

"Minister Snegaddrick," the king said. "What is it?"

"I know I am an outsider here," the ambassador started, "but I must say, a speedy resolution of the situation would be most favorable to our two peoples."

"Please elaborate."

"As Your Majesty is well aware, the marriage of our Prince Gaelyn to your Princess Kathryn was to seal the treaty between our two nations. With Prince Gaelyn's untimely death in your court, I know that the people of Gwythia will want retribution, and swiftly. The death of those involved would show them that your offer of peace was sincere, and guarantee a degree of stability."

"Then I am sure that you will assure your great king and his people that we are most earnest in our search for justice and our deepest condolences."

"I will try, Your Majesty, but perhaps—"

"I will not deny the rights of my loyal subjects, or circumvent the law of this land in an attempt to cater to your sense of prudence, Minister!"

Shouting at the ambassador was a strain on the king and he wheezed himself into a coughing fit, which continued for some time.

"Yes, of course, Your Majesty. My apologies."

"That is all," King William said between coughs.

Ergyfel stepped forward. "As you wish, Your Majesty. Shall I send men to fetch Sir Hugh and Lady Myrredith?"

"I will send a royal page, cousin," the king wheezed.

"Yes, Your Majesty."

A moment later, Billy heard the crowd dispersing. The guards with Billy picked him up and carried him back to his tiny cell in the dungeon.

"So," Billy's companion said, "why are you in here?"

"For the assassination of Princess Kathryn and Prince Gaelyn."

"You killed a prince and a princess?"

"No! But they think I did."

"You didn't do it?"

"Of course not! They were my friends! And now two more of my friends are in danger."

"Well, there's nothin' you can do about it now. Might as well sleep."

Billy wished that the crazy old man were wrong. He so wanted to help his friends. *But how? I can't even help myself!*

Billy mulled over his situation. His thoughts formed circles, always leading him back to his tiny cell. The paths his mind took got shorter and shorter until all his mind could see was the cell—with no way out. Exhausted, Billy finally sank into sleep.

CHAPTER TWENTY-ONE

Dream Time

Billy slept. He did not wish to think on his predicament, and so he slept. In the dark, the hours faded into days, and the days blurred together until time lost all meaning. In his dreams he found escape. He saw himself with his father or Lady Myrredith and Sir Hugh, and sometimes even Sir Aonghas, running across open fields of heather under a bright spring sun.

Then came the nightmare. It perpetually prowled just out of sight, over the hill, or around the next bend. It pounced unpredictably and slashed through his pleasant dreams, cutting them shorter and shorter, until it dominated his dream time.

The nightmare became increasingly vivid with each dreaming, and though it followed the same course, Billy could not force himself to wake. He could never convince himself that it was only a dream.

Over and over again, Sir Hugh saved Billy from the forest dragon, only to turn on him. Hugh chased him, screaming and swinging his sword over his head. The harder Billy tried to outrun Hugh, the closer he got, until Hugh was right on top of him. Then, just as Hugh was about to strike, Billy would wake up, drenched in sweat and bruised from his own thrashing around.

Finally there came a change. The dragon appeared to Billy instantly—before any other dreaming. Hugh slew the dragon and charged Billy. When Billy turned to run from him, instead of a large open field, he found himself in his dungeon cell at Castle Orgulous. Quickly he turned back to look for Sir Hugh, but found only the blackness and a stone wall.

A soft, feminine voice called to him. "William."

Billy spun around. Before him was the dazzling vision of a serene woman wearing a flowing pink and white dress with sparkling jewels. It was the image of his mother; the same image that had led him out of the Cyndyn catacombs. She knelt on the floor, radiating an eerie light that illuminated the tiny room.

"Mother?"

"Yes, William." Her voice was comforting like a lullaby. Billy looked at the ring on his hand. It glowed with a pale blue light.

"Mother, what should I do?"

"Soon, my son, a chance to escape this place will present itself to you. You must take it. It is your only chance."

"What is it?"

"You will know when it is time."

"What about Sir Hugh and Lady Myrredith?"

"Do not think of them. This is your only hope."

"But they are my friends!"

"They will be fine, my son." She reached out, took his hand, and drew him to her breast, her arms enveloping him. "There are others—many others—who are depending on you."

"Depending on *me*?"

"Waiting for you."

Surrounded by the comfort of his mother's arms, Billy's worries eased. He laid his head in her lap, and she caressed his cheek as they gazed at one another.

"Where shall I go, Mother? You once said I would go to Tirn Aill. Shall I seek it out now?"

"Escape this kingdom and go to the Emerald Isle."

"Erin?"

"In time, Tirn Aill will find you. Now sleep."

Billy felt at peace with the world. He closed his eyes and went to sleep. When he awoke, it was because his nameless companion was tugging on his sleeve.

"Billy?" the man whispered. "Billy, are you awake?"

The image of Billy's mother was gone, and the cell was again dark as the abyss.

"I am now!" Billy was perturbed with the interruption of the only good sleep he had received.

"Billy, I want you to take me with you."

"What?"

"When you escape, please take me with you."

Billy sat up and faced the man. Though he couldn't see his companion, he felt his breath and knew he was close. Billy was nervous being that near a mad man. He scooted away and felt his back against the wall. Again the man moved closer, to be directly in front of Billy.

"If I can," Billy said.

"You'll take me with you?"

"I'll take you with me."

"Promise?"

"I promise."

"Good! Shake on it."

Billy felt the man's hand on his chest. He reached up and gripped the hand. Blinding light blasted his vision. At first he thought someone had opened the hatch, but it was much too bright. It was not like the light from a torch or even the sun. This light came from within his mind.

Suddenly Billy saw the queen's garden in Castle Orgulous. A guardsman looked down at the garden from the narrow window just outside the king's chamber. The name Wyte entered Billy's mind, and he knew that this guardsman was the man who now shared his oubliette. The queen was in her garden, near the pond, pleading with her killer. This time around, things were clearer to Billy, but because of the distance and trees, there were few details. A feeling of dread rose within Billy as he watched the tragic incident building to its sadly undeniable conclusion. Billy forced himself to look carefully. He could see the dark figure of Ergyfel behind the trees. *But who is the murderer?* The richly dressed man seemed familiar, but Billy could not see his face.

As before, the man struck the kneeling queen, and Billy felt a heat within his body, within his blood. The murderer grabbed the queen by the throat and throttled her. Billy's blood grew hotter yet, and his pulse quickened.

"No!" Wyte cried.

The next moment, the queen's body lay limp in the killer's hands. Ergyfel came behind the murderer and looked directly up at the window. Billy wanted to hide but felt strangely paralyzed.

Instantly the scene changed. A young Ergyfel stood over Wyte.

"It was your watch," Ergyfel declared. "You are to blame." Then he mumbled a passage of strange words and put his finger to Wyte's forehead. "Forget, forget, forget."

Billy saw Wyte lowered into the tiny oubliette, and the cover dropped. As Ergyfel's words echoed in Billy's mind, his thoughts started to recede and grow dim. It became difficult to maintain focus.

Billy began to feel tired and lost. He was starting to forget. Shivers ran the length of Billy's spine. He shook himself to lose the sensation. Instantly he saw the bright light within his head, followed by pitch darkness. He felt the grip of his cellmate's hand in his, and they shook. Then the man moved away, to the other side of the tiny room.

"Good," the man said. "You'll take Wyte with you."

Billy was dumbfounded by what he had just experienced. "Your name is Wyte?"

"Aye … that's right. Say, I remembered!"

"Wyte, do you remember why you're here?"

There was silence, and then Wyte answered. "No."

"I think *I* know why you're here," Billy said.

"Really? Why?"

"You—"

"No!" Wyte shouted. "I don't want to know."

"But you've done nothing wrong!"

"No! You're one of his imps! Come to torment me. I'm a terrible, evil sinner! That's why I'm here."

"But you're not—!"

"Stop it!" Billy's cellmate shouted. "Please stop it! It hurts." He began to sob. "Please, dear Lord, stop this torment."

Billy backed away from the man, as far as the smelly little cell would allow. Time passed very slowly as Billy waited for his companion to pull himself together.

At last, Billy heard someone coming—armored men in heavy boots. He knew they were coming for him. As he confronted the thought of his impending execution, an unexpected idea popped into his head.

"Quickly, Wyte!" Billy whispered.

"Is this it?" his excited cellmate asked. "Are we escaping?"

"No! ... I mean—maybe—I mean—I don't know."

"Then this isn't it," Wyte declared, obviously deflated.

"Now quickly, Wyte, before they come, tell me how you knew I was escaping!"

"I saw you talking with the pretty lady."

"You saw her?"

"Of course," Wyte said. "And I heard her too."

"Then she's real!" Billy said, as the crack of light around the cell's hatch appeared. "She's real."

CHAPTER TWENTY-TWO

Fate

Billy was brought once more to the king's great hall. It was nighttime, so his eyes were not assaulted by the blinding light of day. Billy kept an eye out for his chance to escape, but he didn't think it could happen while he was bound and under the watchful eye of the guards.

In the middle of their journey, they stopped and put Billy into a small, spherical cage suspended from a long iron pole. Once he was locked inside, they removed his chains and forced him to change into another set of clothes.

Billy's new attire made him wish he could hide. It was made entirely from white and blue diamond-shaped patches raggedly stitched together. One leg of the hideous costume was shorter than the other, as was one sleeve. Lastly, they strapped a ridiculous hat on his head and reinstated his manacles. They never allowed him to remove the gag.

Four guards picked up Billy's cage by the iron pole, while the others picked up the stands. It was clearly heavy, but they never complained. The squad marched on until they came to the small door leading into the king's great hall.

Their captain went in, leaving the door ajar. A moment later, Billy heard Ergyfel's voice over the hubbub inside.

"Sire, I have arranged for some entertainment."

"I hardly think that entertainment is appropriate during this time of mourning, cousin," King William scolded.

"I think you shall change your mind when you see what I have brought for you, Sire."

"Very well, cousin, but be advised: I am not in a forgiving mood."

The captain of the guard poked his head through the door and ordered his men to carry Billy into the great hall. The crowd was still relatively quiet when their prisoner came into view.

A mix of angry cries and laughter exploded from the king's gathered guests. Billy hid his face in the crook of his arm and hoped that the king would be angry enough to send him away.

"Ergyfel ..." the king said in a warning tone.

The King's First Advisor turned to his cousin and bowed deeply. "Your Majesty, your jester is ready."

The guards carried Billy to the left side of King William's dais and set the cage back on its stands. There was a low, grumbling sound from the opposite corner that gave Billy shivers. He looked and saw a troghoul lounging in the shadows under the dais. Billy remembered that the royal hounds had occupied that spot before. The creature growled at him and gnawed on a large bone, snapping it in two.

"There, there, Werian," Ergyfel said to the beast. "He's not going to hurt you."

Then the magister crossed to Billy and spoke to him in a voice just above a whisper. "This can be easy, or very, very difficult. The court is beginning to gather under my banner. They know that I will soon be king. Those that weren't already in my good graces are trying to be. They will all follow my example, like ripples in a pond. Do you understand?"

Billy pondered Ergyfel's words as he surveyed the assembled court. Only the nobility and servants were present now, and though they were each involved in their own conversation or task, their eyes continually gravitated to the king's cousin. Billy also observed that a majority of them wore black or other dark colors. He hoped that it was in deference to

Kathryn and Gaelyn, and not a symptom of Ergyfel's influence. Billy nodded his head.

"Good!" Ergyfel said smugly. "Now if I were to say ... strike you, how do you think they would respond? I'm sure there would be a multitude of responses from them, depending on their individual need to please me. It would be interesting to see who is the more eager. Shall we find out?"

Billy shook his head negatively.

"Good. I find such wasteful shows of power deplorable. Still ..."

Billy fidgeted in his cage, preparing for the worst.

The magister smiled, enjoying Billy's discomfort. "Ah, I see you grow eager. It's so gratifying to know that so many people want to please me. Allow me to lay it out plainly for you. Give me the ring and your last days on earth could be easy. Keep the ring and ... Well, let's just say that I am eager to test the waters."

"Cousin," the king said, addressing Ergyfel's back. "It concerns me, that you take counsel with our jester and not with us. Is there something the matter?"

"No, Your Majesty. I simply wished to impress upon him his position, and the conditions under which he would be allowed to stay in your gracious company."

"I see," the king remarked.

Ergyfel reached into his robes and pulled out three small balls. He held them out to his prisoner, but Billy would not take them.

"You will take these balls and juggle," Ergyfel whispered, "or I shall begin my little experiment in loyalty this instant."

Billy reached through the bars of his cage and took the balls. Using his hands, he indicated that it was too cramped in the cage to juggle. Billy hoped this might get him released.

Ergyfel frowned. "You will just have to juggle through the bars."

Billy straightened his legs and stuck his feet through the bottom of the cage. While sitting, he leaned forward, putting his face between the bars and his hands outside. It was uncomfortable and restricted his movements, but it was only a small inconvenience for Billy's exceptional talents.

Billy juggled the three balls, slowly at first and then more quickly as he grew bored. Juggling usually brought him pleasure, but now he felt none. Even his audience became bored. He continued to juggle, occasionally changing the pattern, and thinking about his escape.

How will it happen? And when?

Out of the blue, Billy was struck by an idea. Immediately he dropped one of the balls. It rolled to Ergyfel who was standing a few feet away, beside Lady Maeven. Ergyfel looked down and picked up the ball. Not wanting to interrupt his conversation, he tossed the ball back to the guard next to Billy's cage, who carefully handed it to Billy. Billy began to juggle again and then purposely let another ball slip. This one he rolled to Maeven's feet. Again Ergyfel bent down, picked up the ball, and returned it. Billy liked the idea of making Ergyfel fetch his "stray" balls, and so, after a short while, he allowed yet another ball to interfere with Ergyfel's politics.

"That is enough!" Ergyfel said angrily.

"Why not let him out of the cage?" said Lady Maeven. "He could fetch for himself."

Ergyfel eyed Billy suspiciously. "Very well," he said, "but he will need to be guarded."

"I will be his keeper." Don Miguel Scarosa appeared from behind a column. He looked exactly as Billy had seen him that first night in Cyndyn Hall—a pompous black bird. The only changes were the absence of his lute and the addition of some stylish black gloves.

Ergyfel eyed the man, and Miguel gave him one of his flamboyant, pretentious bows.

"Don Miguel, would you care to watch our prisoner?"

"My lord." Miguel gave Billy a menacing smile. "It would be my pleasure."

Billy did not like the way Don Miguel stared at him. He liked the idea of being left in his care even less. Billy still remembered his triumph at the royal wedding and was sure that the jealous Scarosa did as well.

Ergyfel instructed the guard to release Billy from his cage and to fasten a collar and chain about his neck. The only such device available had been fashioned for Ergyfel's loathsome pets. Billy recoiled from the putrid troghoul leash until two guards held him while a third fastened it around his throat.

Don Miguel pulled Billy's chain. "Come along, my little pet."

Billy followed Scarosa to the center of the hall. There, the Spaniard sat on a bench and ordered Billy to juggle.

"Juggle, my little monkey."

Billy glared at his keeper. Then, instead of doing the man's bidding, he sat on the floor and crossed his arms.

Scarosa stood and yanked Billy's leash. "Juggle, I say! Juggle!"

Billy was pulled over by Miguel but quickly righted himself and retook his obstinate pose. A number of the nobles and servants giggled.

Don Miguel Scarosa turned beet red as he approached Billy and slapped him on the head. He then pulled Billy up to his knees and kicked him in the seat. "I say to juggle, you little fool, and I meant it!"

Billy still refused, and Miguel pulled him to his feet. The troubadour raised his hand to strike.

"Don Miguel!" the king shouted.

The Spaniard pulled Billy behind him. "Yes, Your Majesty." He then bowed humbly. "I apologize for my monkey, but he will no juggle."

A gaggle of giggles flew from the crowd's lips. Unbeknownst to Don Miguel, Billy had begun juggling behind his back. Even the king chuckled at Billy's joke. Puzzled by this response, Scarosa glanced from side to side. The giggles became laughter. Finally, the Spaniard spun around when he realized he was the butt of a joke emanating from that quarter. Billy instantly stopped juggling. The crowd applauded but quickly fell silent when Scarosa dropped Billy to his knees with a kick to the stomach.

The nobles booed Don Miguel. The more outspoken of the servants hissed. Scarosa looked to Ergyfel, who frowned and held up his hands.

"My gentle lords," the King's First Advisor said, "let us not forget what this ruffian—nay, this villain—has done!"

The guests and servants quieted.

"And our good friend, Don Miguel, who has entertained us with song and good cheer to brighten many a dull night ... Have we forgotten common hospitality?"

Ergyfel approached Billy, who was still doubled over on the floor. He crouched beside him and whispered. "Now boy, I suggest you entertain us with some juggling, or I swear you will entertain us with your execution!"

Billy looked up to Ergyfel's face. The king's cousin stared back at him, frigid as an icicle.

"Tonight!" Ergyfel stood and walked away.

Billy dragged himself up to his feet. He held his side and stared after the magister until Don Miguel pulled on his chain. Billy then turned his attention to the Spaniard, whose lips quivered in restraint of a smile.

Billy, despite his desire to do otherwise, began to juggle. Again there was no pleasure in it for him. Don Miguel took every opportunity to humiliate him. First Scarosa would trip Billy, then make him search for the lost balls on all fours like a dog. When Billy tired, Miguel kicked him in the rear to keep him moving. Most of those present, not wishing to appear sympathetic, hid their faces and tried to focus away from this deplorable activity. There were, however, those who enjoyed Billy's torment and even participated in it. Billy wondered whether they were eager to earn points with Ergyfel or just plain hateful.

"There's a good little freak," Don Miguel said as Billy retrieved one of the dropped balls.

Billy felt angry, humiliated, and frightened all at once. He started to think about his impending execution. There seemed to be nothing he could do to prevent it. In truth, some part of him began to wish for the release it would bring. It presented a kind of escape.

In the vision, his mother had said his chance for escape would come soon. *If this is what she meant, then let it be soon.*

The word "soon" echoed in his head. It caught painfully in his dry throat as if he had tried to speak it. Tears flowed down his face as he choked on the dusty taste of his fate.

Two feet stepped into view before Billy. He didn't care whose feet they were.

I'll attack them, and confound Ergyfel if he wants to execute me!

Billy prepared to pounce on the legs and scratch them until they bled.

And if I can get my gag out ...

"Your Majesty," Don Miguel said from behind Billy.

Your Majesty?

Billy's mind was so focused that the words sounded foreign. It took a moment for their meaning to register.

Billy's eyes followed the legs upward. He came to a man's withered hand with a large signet ring upon it. His eyes continued up the man's body until they came to the face of his king.

Anger and hatred did not mask King William's face, as Billy expected, but rather sorrow. His tired blue eyes looked into Billy's with an expression of regret. Billy noticed wetness welling up in the king's eyes.

Without warning, King William reached out and gently touched Billy's cheek where tears had made it wet. It was the same way John had done when Billy scraped his knee, or some other childhood hurt had caused him to cry. With childlike innocence, he reached up and touched the king's hand. In that instant, Billy saw the bright white light and knew that he was entering the strange world of memories.

Once again, when the brightness cleared, Billy found himself in the queen's garden. He watched as the king entered the garden with Ergyfel on his heels. The king gritted his teeth and gripped the sword at his side. As he turned the corner at the far end of the garden, he pointed a finger and shouted in a surprisingly clear voice.

"Eleanor!"

Billy jumped, startled by the volume and clarity of the king's voice. It was a shock that drew Billy further into the vision.

A sweet, melodic voice answered. "Yes, my husband."

Billy turned to look at the queen. His brain came to a jarring stop when he saw Queen Eleanor's face. It was the face he had come to know as his mother's. The king shouted something, and the queen answered, but Billy didn't hear them. He was still staring at Eleanor's face. Then, as a hammer struck to an anvil, Billy's mind rang with the truth that his mother was indeed Queen Eleanor; his father, King William. The enormity of this revelation was too much for Billy. An endless cascade of questions and emotions washed through and over him, causing a shudder from deep within like an angry, primal scream.

Billy's mind returned to the scene, which seemed determined to play itself out to its unforgettable, unalterable end. In the back of his head he continued to wrestle with his newfound identity. It refashioned his view of the world and his place in it. This new role gave him special purpose, which he also knew was as immutable as the past—as unswerving as the fate that brought him to Castle Orgulous and to the discovery of many incredible secrets. There was nothing done which he could undo. All that remained was to accept what was on his plate and push forward.

"Where is my son, woman?" King William shouted. "You've killed him, haven't you?"

"No, my lord!"

"Then what have you done with him, harlot!"

"My King ..." pleaded Billy's mother, kneeling before her husband.

"What have you done?"

"Our son is safe, my lord."

"You've stolen him!" King William spat. "You've taken him to your people, haven't you? Haven't you?"

"I've not left Orgulous, my lord!"

"You've betrayed me!"

"No!"

"Liar!"

The king struck Eleanor, bashing her to the ground. Billy's stomach twisted in knots. The vision was so real that he felt he was part of it, but he was unable to affect anything.

Mother! Mother!

For a moment King William hesitated. To his horror, Billy could only watch as the king swooped down and wrapped his hands around his mother's throat. Billy became dizzy and nauseous. His mind filled with the blinding white light, and he felt himself return to the world of the present.

Pain shot through Billy's hand as the flat of a sword knocked it away from the king. His stomach was still churning, and he felt what little food he had eaten coming back up. He grabbed his gag and ripped it from his lips.

When Billy's head and stomach stopped spinning, he looked up and saw the king dolefully staring at him. Billy was sick at heart as he considered his country's ruler. The man whom he had loved—the hero he had admired—instantly reduced to a loathsome murderer. Billy had never felt so confused or trapped.

You killed my mother. But Ergyfel...

Billy was filled with hatred and pity; hatred for the man who had killed his mother, pity for the king who had fallen victim to scheming and sorcery. Both emotions, like branding irons, burned themselves into Billy's heart. His entire body ached from wanting to fold in on itself. Tears of anguish flowed from his eyes.

"It was you ..." he croaked hoarsely.

* * *

Billy awoke with a headache that started in his toes. It was dark and cramped, so he believed he must be back in his cell. Then he heard a familiar voice.

"Billy. Billy."

Billy squinted. It was definitely not his cell, as it was far too light, and Gryff's face was before him. Billy blinked away the haziness and saw that he was back inside the small spherical cage, still in the king's great hall. He started to speak, but his gag was also back in place.

"I've come to help you," Gryff whispered.

Billy scanned the hall. Most of the noble guests had left, while some few had remained to drink themselves into a stupor and pass out. Their sleeping, snoring bodies lay draped over the tables, giving the impression of a gruesome battlefield.

Quietly, Gryff fit a key into the cage's lock and opened it. Once Billy had climbed out, they removed his manacles.

"Shhh," Gryff warned as Billy removed his gag.

"I wasn't gonna say anythin'," Billy whispered.

"Good, but—"

Someone grunted directly behind them, and they spun around. A man sat with his hands wrapped around a tankard and a dull, glazed expression on his face. He grunted again.

"Milord!" Gryff bowed quickly. "I was just-just … taking the prisoner back to his cell."

The man remained still, staring straight ahead. He took a deep breath and grunted.

Both Gryff and Billy froze, waiting for the nobleman to do or say something. Time passed slowly. Again the man inhaled deeply and grunted.

Billy cautiously stepped forward, watching for a reaction from the lord. There was none. Then he took another step, and another, until he was just inches from the man's face. Billy then waved his hand before the noble's eyes. The only reaction was another grunt. Billy jumped back and held his breath. He waited for a moment before pulling on his cheeks and making faces at the man, all with no response.

"He's asleep!" Billy whispered.

Gryff approached. "Never seen anyone sleep with his eyes open. Gives me the hives. Come on. No tellin' how long he'll be sleepin' it off. We better get movin'."

Gryff took Billy by the hand and quietly led him to a corner behind the dais of the king's great hall. There he pushed on a stone, and a small passage opened behind the nearest tapestry.

"A secret door!" Billy hissed.

"Shhh!" Gryff pulled Billy through the opening. He then closed the stone door and lit a lamp. "Not many know 'bout this one," he said softly, "an' I only know 'bout it by chance."

Gryff led Billy by the hand through the narrow, dark passage. They continued down several flights of steps and then entered a long, twisting tunnel with an arched ceiling. The floor was damp and slimy, the air close. The dank odor and appearance reminded Billy of the catacombs under Cyndyn Hall. He became anxious and felt trapped, but before the feeling could overwhelm him, they came to another set of steps. At the top of the steps there was a ladder.

Gryff climbed up the ladder. As he reached the top, he blew out the lamp, leaving Billy in the dark. Then Billy saw Gryff silhouetted against a small cluster of stars.

"Come on, Billy."

Billy rapidly climbed the ladder. As he reached the top, he saw a rock rolled to the side. He inhaled the cool, clean night air and looked into the sparkling sky.

As Gryff helped him to his feet, Billy saw the pale outer walls of Castle Orgulous bathed in the light of the quarter moon. They stood in a small clearing surrounded by a dense bramble a short distance from the great castle. Billy remembered the first time he had seen Orgulous. He had been filled with the joy of expectation and curiosity. It had embodied a lifelong dream. Now it represented a nightmare, and the last place on earth he wanted to be.

"Wyte!" Billy said, remembering the cellmate he left behind.

"What?"

"I promised Wyte I'd take him with me."

"Ya can't help him, Billy."

Billy chewed on his lip. "I know."

Just then, there was movement in the brush and a heavy sound on the ground. Billy scanned the edge of the tiny clearing and saw a horse grazing near a tree, saddled and ready to ride.

Gryff walked Billy to the mount. "I packed a few things for you in the bags. Dana sent you some victuals for the road as well."

As Billy got close to the animal he recognized it as Briallen, Prince Gaelyn's horse. "I can't take her!"

"Why not?"

"She's the prince's horse!"

"Look lad, Prince Gaelyn would have given her to you himself, had he been able. I'm sure of it."

Billy mounted Briallen and took the reins from Gryff. "It's a good thing the prince taught me a little about his riding style." He sat back in the saddle and took a hard look at the man who had saved him from certain death. He was a plain, honest man. One who befriended a strange boy, took him in, listened to him, and trusted him. Now certainly, he put his life on the line for him.

If he only knew who I really am ... Billy felt the wheels of fate turn once again. "How can I ever repay you, my friend?"

"Escape," Gryff answered. "Get away from this place. Live. That will be my reward."

Billy leaned over and clasped Gryff on the arm. They stared at each other's face, knowing there were still many dangers ahead for them both.

Gryff broke away. "Now hurry!"

Billy nodded and Gryff swatted Briallen on the rear. The regal mare and her small rider sped down the only path from the clearing and were swallowed up by the darkness.

Gryff looked up into the starry sky and sighed. "Lord, keep Your hand on the lad. Guide him to safety ... and give me the strength to do what I must."

CHAPTER TWENTY-THREE

The Hunt Begins

Sir Hugh rode up the King's Road to Nyraval. He had parted company with Lady Myrredith only two days previously, having reluctantly left her in the care of Earl Finney's guardsmen and Malcolm the Magnificent.

The king's messenger had caught up to Aonghas' funeral procession two days out of Hillshire. The uncommonly quiet page handed Hugh the king's summons and then refused to comment, other than to say that he was to return with Hugh to Castle Orgulous.

"What is the meaning of this?" Lady Myrredith asked. "Surely the king knows that Sir Hugh is escorting me back to Dyven."

"I cannot say," the page answered.

Hugh looked up from the summons. "What has happened? Why does the king need me so 'urgently'?"

"I cannot say."

"What is your name, boy?"

"Luke, sir."

"Luke, you must tell me what happened. Is there trouble?"

"I was instructed to say nothing."

"By whom?"

Luke bowed to Lady Myrredith. "By the King's First Counselor, milady."

"Ergyfel!" Hugh, Myrredith and Malcolm exclaimed.

The page blushed and nervously stepped towards his horse.

"I thought I smelled a snake," Malcolm muttered.

Myrredith nodded. "He's up to something."

"Aye," Hugh said. "He wouldn't want me back there unless he was ready to play an extraordinary move."

Malcolm raised an eyebrow. "Move?"

"The magister and I are playing a chess game of sorts."

"Then he must hope to declare cyning daith."

Hugh's face fell. "King's death. Let's hope not."

Myrredith put her hand on his arm. "Hugh, don't go."

"I must. It is my king who calls."

"I will go with you."

"No, milady. You must bury your husband. So far, the king is only interested in me."

"Perhaps you'd fancy my company?" Malcolm offered.

"I can handle Ergyfel. I need you to see to Lady Myrredith's safety."

"Aye. That I will do."

In this fashion, Sir Hugh found himself in the company of Luke, the close-lipped page, a mere half day's ride from his king. Luke had remained amazingly steadfast to his oath of silence, and Hugh did not press him. The King's Champion knew what it was to be a page. He remembered the tremendous pressures to perform and the constant scrutiny. However, Luke was taking the whole thing far too strictly. He never engaged Hugh in conversation except to answer the most perfunctory of questions and give courteous thanks. It was as if the boy were afraid to speak, lest an open mouth betray some terrible secret. This greatly troubled Hugh. The last time someone had approached him with such trepidation it was to tell him of his mother's death.

As Hugh spurred Splendore on towards Orgulous, he pondered what secret lurked in the mind of the boy riding next to him. The sound of approaching horses interrupted his thoughts. Hugh looked up the road and saw three of his fellow knights rounding the bend at top speed.

"Whoa, Splendore!" Hugh brought his mount to a stop.

The knights continued down the road and stopped a few yards ahead of Hugh. Sir Owein greeted the King's Champion as the dust settled.

"Hail, Sir Hugh."

"Hail, Owein." Hugh smiled and nodded to the other two knights. "Gareth, Darn. Where is it you go in such a hurry, my friends?"

"*Friends* he says."

"Darn!" Owein shot the knight a warning glance.

Hugh inspected the three men, taking note of the unusual distance between them and the defensive posture that each of them had taken. "Aye, friends," he said. He edged his horse forward, narrowing the gap between them. "For what reason should I not address such good comrades as *friends*?"

Sir Owein spoke to Luke. "He doesn't know?"

Hugh looked at the page. "Know what?"

"No, Sir Owein."

Again Owein addressed the messenger. "You didn't tell him?"

"No sir."

"Tell me what?" Hugh asked.

Sir Owein eyed Hugh then moved his horse in close beside Splendore. "Princess Kathryn and Prince Gaelyn are dead."

"What?"

"Murdered by an assassin."

Hugh could say nothing. His mind reeled, as did his body. He started to fall from his horse. At the last second, Sir Owein grabbed his arm, steadying him. Hugh closed his eyes and swallowed hard. There was an ache in his chest, an empty, heavy anguish he had not felt since the day he lost Myrredith to Aonghas. A torrent of tears threatened to flood his eyes, but disbelief kept them in check.

Owein leaned closer and spoke softly to his shaken comrade. "That is not all, my brother."

Hugh swallowed again and straightened his back. His entire body stiffened, bracing for another blow.

"Billy stands accused."

"No!"

"Ergyfel's got evidence—"

"It's a lie!"

"Don't you think I know—that I want to believe—but I-I don't know what to believe. The evidence—"

"It's a lie, I tell you! A lie! If it came from Ergyfel, you can be sure of it!"

"Regardless, Hugh," Darn said, "the king has pronounced his judgment, and we have all been sent to catch him."

"Catch who?"

Owein frowned. "Billy escaped sometime during the night."

"From Orgulous?"

"Aye," Gareth said.

"And the king has sent you three to catch him?"

Darn drank from a skin then said, "Not just we three."

Gareth took the skin from Darn. "Ergyfel commissioned all the knights in Orgulous."

"Ergyfel?" Hugh looked to Owein for confirmation.

"Yes, Ergyfel."

"Since when does Ergyfel command the king's knights?"

Owein squeezed Hugh's arm. "The king's illness has worsened tremendously."

"Yes, I'll bet it has," Hugh spat, "and I know just who's responsible for that!"

Hugh jerked his arm away from Sir Owein's grasp and prepared to speed away to Castle Orgulous. Before he could move, Owein grabbed him again.

"My friend, my friend, my brother!" Owein said, forcing Hugh to look at him. "Let me give you a warning. I know what you're thinking, and you had better get that idea out of your head right now!"

Hugh gritted his teeth and stared at his friend. Sir Owein was taken aback by the feral look in Hugh's eyes.

Calm, yet firmly, Sir Owein continued. "Things are different than you might expect, my friend—my brother. The balance of the court has already shifted in favor of Ergyfel. You will not be given your usual due."

Hugh regained some of his composure. "I am the King's Champion. If I do not confront the magister, then who will?"

"Hugh, because of our friendship, I must give you yet another warning. Billy does not stand charged alone."

"What do you mean?"

"Ergyfel has implied … that you and Lady Myrredith might have—"

Hugh's face reddened at the mention of Myrredith. He snapped his arm away from Owein and swatted Splendore with the reins. Instantly, the high-spirited steed charged away, leaving the three knights and page flat-footed in the road.

As the worried page hurried after his charge, Sir Owein shouted after them. "Hugh! Arm yourself with reason! With reason!"

Owein, Gareth, and Darn waited in the road a moment, watching Sir Hugh and Luke disappear around the curve. They looked at each other solemnly.

Owein shook his head. "Come. We three distinguished knights of the realm have a small boy to catch … and unfortunately, I think I know where he's headed."

CHAPTER TWENTY-FOUR

On Fate's Path

Billy rode like never before, pushing himself beyond his limits. Briallen, Prince Gaelyn's horse, gave him her all, responding to her new rider like an old friend. The prince would have been proud.

To Erin, but first home. The instant he made this decision, he felt oddly torn. *I must fetch Father, so we can go to the Emerald Isle together.* However, something within him advised against it—urging him instead to go straight to Erin. At first it was a queer, uneasy feeling, and he shrugged it off as a case of nerves, but then it grew stronger and seemed to speak to him. He listened, and without warning he heard his mother's voice.

Stay away from that place, said the voice. *It isn't safe. Go directly to the Emerald Isle.*

Gradually Billy realized that it was his mother's ring trying to warn him away. He focused on the strange thoughts it projected into his consciousness until he bridled them to his will.

"We are going home," he stated aloud, "and that's final!"

There was no more dissension. There were, however, quiet warnings. Several times Billy felt a prickling on the back of his neck and got off the road. Each time, a moment would pass, and then someone would come up the road. In this way, he managed to avoid any contact, but waiting in hiding and traveling so cautiously slowed his progress.

Billy decided to stay away from the main roads and travel under the cover of darkness. He wasn't sure which way to go, having journeyed through this country only once in his life. Also, traveling at night made navigation nearly impossible. However, Billy kept his mind focused on John and the Valley of the Yew. The ring did the rest.

It wasn't easy to let go and allow the ring to guide him, but after a short while, he learned to trust it. He also began to believe in destiny, which seemed determined to map out the path for his life whether he liked it or not.

When he wasn't concentrating on home, Billy wrestled with his new identity. Accepting King William as his father could have been easy, and in some ways wonderful, if the king wasn't also his mother's murderer. He felt the urge to cut out the part of him that came from his father, but of course this was impossible.

Billy felt betrayed. He hated King William. It didn't matter that his father had been under the influence of Ergyfel's magic. A hero such as King William was *supposed to be beyond the reach of such evil, but he was weak!*

Most of all, Billy hated his new identity as the *son of a murderer*. It was the first time in his life that he truly hated something about himself. In time, Billy had come to accept his imperfect body, but this was not something he could just learn to tailor around. It was too important—too reprehensible—to ignore. Billy knew he could not change the past, but he felt that if he were to live with himself, he would have to set his father's wrongs to right. The question was, *how?*

One night, as Billy crossed over a ridge, the light of a campfire struck his eyes. He reined Briallen to a stop. At the bottom of the hill lay the King's Road. A small caravan camped beside the road, made up of two wagons and a number of horses. The entire entourage was clad in black, including the wagons. Several men slept around a fire in the center of the camp, while others kept watch. Billy was about to turn Briallen and go quietly around the camp when he spotted Malcolm the Magnificent. The last time Billy had seen his mentor was in the company of Lady Myrredith, as she left for Hillshire. In answer to his thoughts, Myrredith appeared from one of the wagons. Billy dismounted and quietly worked his way down the hill.

Billy came up behind the horse line, remaining hidden in the bushes. He scanned the area to get the position of the guards and then turned his attention to Myrredith.

"Where do you think he is?" Lady Myrredith asked Malcolm.

The juggling master uncrossed his arms and looked away from the fire. "In Orgulous, I imagine."

"I hope ..."

"Don't worry, milady. Hugh can take care of himself."

Billy searched for Splendore Pomponnel. The horse and its rider were nowhere to be seen.

"I wonder what could have been so important." Myrredith asked.

"The king's messenger wasn't very informative," Malcolm complained.

"Aye. That's what worries me."

"Try not to let it trouble you."

"When Aonghas is buried I must go back."

"To Orgulous?"

"Yes. I have the feeling I'm needed there."

"We've made good time. We reach Dyven day after tomorrow. If you will allow me, I would accompany you back."

Lady Myrredith looked at the juggling master for a moment, considering his offer. "Why, Malcolm?"

"I beg your pardon, milady."

"Why are you going out of your way for me?"

"Out of my way? Oh, no! I was goin' back to Orgulous already."

"Oh?"

"Yes. The king seemed to appreciate my talents more than I imagined he would."

"He did reward you rather well. There's no other reason why you wish to go back?"

"Your Ladyship," Malcolm said, "I have traveled most of my life, performing here and there, for king and commoner alike. I have made many friends in my journeys, but ..."

"But what?"

"Please excuse my forwardness, milady, but I have never felt a kinship to anyone, like I feel for you and Sir Hugh, and of course Billy."

Myrredith smiled. "I miss William too."

"He's more than my best student. He's the son I never had."

Myrredith laughed.

"What is it?"

"Your feelings of kinship is not groundless, for Billy has also filled in the place of the brother I lost so many years ago."

"Then in spirit, milady, we are kin."

"Quite. What's more, as soon as Kathryn assumes the throne, Billy will legally become a Cyndyn, and my brother."

Malcolm looked shocked. "Does he know?"

Lady Myrredith nodded. "Malcolm, please forgive me. I shouldn't have questioned your motives. It's just that, Hugh told me how you slew that giant, and then this mysterious summons, and ... I guess I'm just being suspicious. I apologize."

Malcolm bowed his head. "No apology needed, milady. I too have been *on edge*, since Sir Hugh's departure."

Lady Myrredith and her companion fell silent. Billy so wanted to come forward and tell them everything. He wanted to warn them away from Orgulous, but he knew that he could not. To show himself would put them all in worse danger.

"Well, good night," Lady Myrredith said at last.

"Good night, milady."

Billy watched them walk to opposite ends of the camp, and then stole to Lady Myrredith's wagon. While she conversed with Rhianna, he crept into the wagon and retrieved some parchment and writing implements. He then slunk away from the camp and wrote Myrredith a letter.

"Lady Myrredith," it read, "It pains me to inform you that Princess Kathryn and Prince Gaelyn have been murdered. Ergyfel was behind it and has also poisoned King William. The king still holds on, but the court is rallying to Ergyfel. Your friend Billy has been wrongly accused of the crimes, but do not fear, for he has escaped. You must be very careful. Ergyfel has tried to blame you and Sir Hugh too. He will stop at nothing to gain the throne. Castle Orgulous is too dangerous for you. For your safety, and the safety of the kingdom, do not go there!" Billy signed the letter, "Your friend."

Billy folded the letter and tiptoed back to the wagon, using all his stalking skills to remain undetected. Lady Myrredith was now inside, so he very carefully laid the letter on the seat of the wagon and placed a rock on top of it. Then once again, he silently skulked into the trees.

Billy found Briallen exactly where he had left her. He quickly led her around the camp and mounted. As he gave a last glance to the campsite in the valley below, he realized this might be the last time he ever saw Lady Myrredith.

"Take me away from here," he whispered to Briallen.

The mare obligingly trotted over the hill, disappearing with her rider into a forest of shadows.

CHAPTER TWENTY-FIVE

War

Sir Hugh stormed into Castle Orgulous a full hour ahead of Luke. Despite the warnings of Owein, Hugh did not allow wisdom to alter his disposition. Instead, his temper had raged hotter with each league he covered. By the time he crossed through the gates of Orgulous he was a conflagration out of control. Attempts to stop or delay him were swept aside—insignificant as dry leaves to a hurricane.

Hugh burst into King William's great hall unannounced. The two giant doors slammed open with a mighty crash that turned every head. Hugh marched into the hall, as some would say later, "a man possessed."

"Ergyfel!" Hugh shouted as he crossed the long hall to the dais. His face was a mass of taught, grim sinew.

Not a word was spoken as noble and servant alike made way for Hugh's advance. His movements were strong, fluid and sure as an angry lion. Beneath the ridge of his scowling forehead, his wrathful eyes bore through any who were before him. He made a baleful, fearsome sight.

Suddenly Hugh stopped. His posture stiffened, and his face changed to an expression of disbelief. Then his angry mask reappeared, and his hand slapped the hilt of his sword. "How dare you sit on the king's throne?"

All eyes flashed to Ergyfel who lounged in King William's throne.

Coolly, the magister shifted his position and returned Sir Hugh's stare. "It is you, Sir Hugh, who dares much."

"You are the king's counselor—"

"And his heir!"

"But you are still not king!"

"Not *yet*, Champion," the magister said, "but while he is ill I speak for him and will act for him."

"Get off the throne, Ergyfel!"

Ergyfel's left eye squinted as he glared at the King's Champion. "Very well," he said, standing. "If it will make you happy, I will oblige."

Sir Hugh stared levelly at Ergyfel. "Where is the king?"

"He is resting."

Hugh turned and scanned the room, looking into the faces of the lords present. "Where is your king?" he asked. "Only the king can call a council of the lords." He stopped when he came to the ambassador from Gwythia, who had been speaking when Hugh interrupted the court.

"Ambassador Snegaddrick," Hugh said with a curt bow, "I'm sure the king will hear your petition, when he personally reconvenes his court."

The sanctimonious ambassador stepped forward. "Nicely done, Sir Hugh, but I do not think you speak for your countrymen. After all, *you* are implicated in the murders!"

Hugh's grip tightened on his sword. "The charges are false, and I will challenge any man who says otherwise."

"The evidence is rather convincing—"

"Snegaddrick!" Hugh grabbed the pudgy man by the front of his tunic. "If you were a man ..."

"Are you *threatening* me?"

Hugh released the ambassador and turned to face the assembled lords. "I claim trial by combat, as is my right." He then threw a gauntlet to the stone floor. "Is there any among you who would care to press the charges? Any who would put forth a champion to face me before the Lord?"

"How dare you place your hands on me?" Snegaddrick spouted.

Hugh ignored the ambassador and stared at the face of each lord present. Many turned their faces away or hung their heads. Only a few could give Hugh their eyes.

"I've never been so insulted in all my life!" Snegaddrick squawked.

"I doubt that," Hugh said, still showing the ambassador his back.

Ambassador Snegaddrick spat and sputtered. He turned and scurried to the exit. "Sir Hugh!" he managed to shout when he reached the doors. "You ... This is war!"

Hugh glanced at the ambassador. "Oh ... I thought you were going to say something important."

Snegaddrick shook with anger. His face became radish red. Then he grunted and marched out of the hall.

Some of the lords snickered at the ambassador's exit. Some were agitated and cried out for him to stop. Hugh remained calm, giving Snegaddrick no more thought than he would an insect. He looked down at the gauntlet resting on the floor, untouched.

"I expect never again to hear of this lie." Hugh picked up his gauntlet.

"Not so fast," the magister said.

"What is it, Ergyfel?"

"Besides the fact that you've just thrown us back into a war with Gwythia ...?"

"That fat, preposterous snake, is no more capable of starting a war than he is of stopping one. It's only a matter of time before Gwythia invades again. With Prince Gaelyn slain, nothing will dissuade them from their bloody revenge."

"He's right," Hugh heard from the crowd of lords.

"Quite true, Hugh," Ergyfel said. "I had no idea you were so well versed in politics."

"The politics of the battlefield. You forget the many times I've had to fight them."

"Well, there is still the small matter of your possible involvement in the murders."

Hugh said nothing, but tossed the gauntlet at Ergyfel's feet. He then stood back and crossed his arms.

Ergyfel eyed the glove momentarily and then looked to Hugh. "Don't be ridiculous, Sir Hugh. You are the King's Champion. I am the king's heir. Besides, there isn't a man in the kingdom who would dream of taking up arms against you."

"Then bring someone from another kingdom!"

Ergyfel stroked his chin. "An interesting idea, but that isn't the point."

"Then what is?"

"Your martial prowess is well known. What knight or warrior could best you in single combat?"

"If I were guilty, my crimes would hang like great stones about my neck. Without the Lord's strength, I could not be victorious."

"I'm afraid I don't share your faith in that notion. It's far too untested."

"King William established the trial by combat himself."

"That may be so, but as I stated before, no one will fight you."

"Then as the King's Marshal, I will lead the army into battle against Gwythia, and prove my loyalty in the field."

Ergyfel shook his head. "No. There's too much at stake. If you falter, so might our army."

"I thought you didn't believe in trial by combat."

"I don't, but it's a notion I've seen spreading like your faith. With a commander whose resolve is in doubt, the men would have all the morale of frightened sheep. If something unforeseen were to occur, and it was misinterpreted ... No. You must not lead the army."

"I think King William should decide that, don't you?"

One of the lords said, "Yes."

Then another said, "Let the king decide."

Ergyfel hesitated and finally nodded. "Very well, if His Majesty will grant you command of his army—"

"My lords," Hugh said, "make preparations for war."

"When we return," Ergyfel added, "we will announce the king's decision." Then he and Sir Hugh turned and left the king's great hall.

* * *

Hugh entered the royal suite first. King William was resting in bed, his nurse sitting beside him. Hugh's jaw went slack when he saw the king. The great ruler's pale skin had a bluish tint and seemed to be drawn over his bones like wet, wrinkled parchment.

The king mumbled and thrashed sporadically, as if fighting off some creature in his dreams. Hugh looked to the nurse, who shook her head and said, "He hasn't sleep well for years."

Hugh knelt at the side of the bed and waited while Ergyfel sauntered into a dark corner. The nurse nodded, then Hugh reached out and gently gripped the king's hand. "My King. My King, it is I, your servant, Hugh."

The king's eyelids fluttered and slowly opened. "Hugh?"

His champion bowed his head. "Yes, Your Majesty."

"What are you doing here? You should be halfway to Cyndyn Hall."

"Sire, you summoned me."

"I did?" The king nodded off. Then suddenly, he opened his eyes. "Oh yes, I did."

Hugh scooted closer. "Your Majesty, I'm afraid I have hurried us on our way to war again with Gwythia."

"Snegaddrick?"

Hugh nodded his head.

The king gave Hugh a weak smile. "Did you kill him?"

"No, Your Majesty, but I must confess I was tempted."

"Do not confess to me, Hugh." King William coughed. "I'm no priest. Besides, I too have felt that desire."

"What?"

"Oh, many times, my boy. And in my reckless youth … I'm afraid I would have killed him."

Hugh gripped the king's hand and smiled.

"War was inevitable, Hugh."

"Yes, but you have worked so hard to—"

"You know," King William said, "each morning, when I awake, I find I cannot remember with any certainty the events of the previous day, happy or sad. Despite this *vacancy*, for which I should feel nothing, I am descended upon by a black melancholy, but for what I haven't a clue.

"The past is often cloudy, but occasionally I remember a few days from my youth. Those were bold days, my boy!" The king wheezed and stared across the room as if looking across time. Then he grinned. "I remember my first battle, first girl I ever loved, my mother, my queen ..." The king's voice trailed off, and his teary eyes fixed on Hugh. "And your father."

"You remember my father?"

"Oh yes," King William answered. "Your father was a great knight." The king's eyes drooped and then closed. "Some days my right hand reaches out, on its own accord, expecting to find him."

"But still he was torn down by accusations of treason," Hugh muttered.

King William's eyes popped open. "Your father? He would never ..." Then his eyes closed again.

"Then allow me to clear his name and my own by trial."

"Trial?"

"Trial by combat, Your Majesty. It is my right to ask it, and I know the Lord will grant me the strength to defeat these lies once and for all."

The king was half asleep. "No, no. You must lead my army."

Ergyfel appeared beside Hugh. "I do not believe that is wise, Majesty."

The king opened one eye. "Wise, cousin?"

"No, Your Majesty. First, Hugh must clear his name. An army will not follow a man whose piety is clouded."

"But if no one will grant me trial by combat, how can I clear my name?"

Ergyfel tilted his head to one side. "To prove your fealty ... you could bring back the boy."

Hugh stiffened. "Bring back Billy?"

"Preferably, his head!"

"Yes," the king said, looking at his champion with drowsy eyes.

Hugh glanced at the nurse, whose face blanched. Her wide eyes stared unbelieving at her sickly master.

The king took a deep breath. "Bring back Billy." Then his eyes closed, and he sank back into his pillow. "I miss that boy."

Hugh shook the king. "Your Majesty. Your Majesty!"

The king did not stir but mumbled, "Clear your name, Hugh."

"Your Majesty!"

Ergyfel stood tall and raised his chin. "You heard him. Kill the boy."

"That's not what he meant!" Hugh made eye contact with the nurse, who nervously looked away.

"Oh, I think it was," Ergyfel attested.

"The king said to bring him back, but I will not kill him!"

"Then bring the boy back alive. But if he is killed, bring back his ring, and we will accept this as proof that he is dead."

"His ring?" Hugh said.

"That simple, gold band he wears. I will know it."

Hugh bowed his head over the king. "And you will proclaim to all that I am innocent?"

"Yes."

"And Lady Myrredith?"

"Yes, and your father too."

Hugh's head came up, and he looked into Ergyfel's eyes. He stared at their blackness, trying to ascertain the magister's truthfulness.

Ergyfel raised a single finger and leaned towards Hugh. "But fail ..."

Although he might finally clear his father's name and clear himself and Myrredith of all charges, Hugh was set upon by a heavy heart. "Either way, I fear my soul is lost," he muttered.

"What is it to be?"

Hugh glared at his nemesis. "I will do my duty."

"Good." Ergyfel turned and lead Hugh from the king's suite. "Now, before you leave on your quest, you and I must announce to the lords who will be marshal of the army."

"They can decide amongst themselves."

Ergyfel turned to face Hugh. "No! They will bicker and fight until the enemy is pounding down the Glittering Gate. You must help me choose."

Hugh was taken aback by Ergyfel's need for his input. "Why me?"

Ergyfel smiled. "I'm afraid I was a rather poor student when it came to the art of war, but you … you know who can lead us to victory. Besides, I know if you name your successor, they will readily accept him."

"The Earl of Hillshire."

"What? That old man?"

"'That old man' has fought the Gwythies since time began. His experience and cunning will be worth more than a thousand knights."

Ergyfel seemed to weigh Hugh's suggestion while they walked to the great hall. As they reached the side entrance, he stopped and turned to Hugh. "The Earl of Hillshire" was all he said.

* * *

That day, as the Ambassador of Gwythia quietly and unceremoniously left Castle Orgulous, there was no one to bid him "good journey." Moreover, all who passed by Snegaddrick in the gates were in a bigger hurry to leave than he. He counted two dozen royal messengers and nearly as many lords. Not a single citizen of Lyonesse spoke to him as they rushed by. It was as if he were invisible, or a ghost. The thought whipped shivers up his spine. Every dark corner became a murder hole, stuffed with cold-blooded assassins.

Snegaddrick swatted his mount and galloped through the cavernous gatehouse of Orgulous at top speed. Half a league passed under the hooves of his horse before the ambassador slowed to a trot and allowed his small bodyguard to catch up. Each man sat his saddle uneasily and scrutinized the woods along the road. Something unseen was stalking them. The sweaty ambassador felt its chilling breath in the wind and heard its drum-like voice in the thunder of the horses' hooves. And while it did not show its face, the ambassador knew its name, for he had called it forth.

CHAPTER TWENTY-SIX

Homecoming

As evening slipped on her shadowy gown, Billy crossed over the ridge of Cleddyf Point to look down at the Valley of the Yew. He was exhausted and hungry, having ridden the past few days straight through, pausing only long enough for Briallen to rest and water.

Some unknown force, beyond the power of the ring and his need to see John, had driven him. It had crept up on him one night as he crossed a stream in a downpour. In the hiss of the raindrops he heard a whisper, "Hurry, hurry! There isn't much time." In the days that followed, the dead leaves under Briallen's hooves seemed to say, "Quickly now, quickly."

Billy strained to see The Valley's Finest Inn. In the dim light he spotted a wisp of smoke over the distant knoll and hurried from the bare hilltop into the trees.

"Father will be cooking dinner about now," he told Briallen. "And for you, there's always fresh oats in the barn, and maybe an apple."

Carefully, Billy picked his way down the hills into the valley and skirted the fields surrounding the village. He peered through the trees of the hollow and caught glimpses of light, coming from familiar windows, beckoning him to come closer.

The cool darkness of night was heralded by the distant barking of a dog and welcomed by the howls of her fellows. Billy turned his attention to the road. It felt oddly vacant. Even when his father had no guests in his beds, he always managed to have visitors, up for an evening drink or occasional meal, and yet no one traveled the road.

Cautiously, he approached the inn through the woods. He could hear no sounds nor see any lights from the inn. Billy thought for a moment that he had lost his way, and then suddenly the woods ended. A large, barren circle of blackened earth and burnt trees stretched before him. Roughly in the center of the strangely naked ebon trees lay a heap of charred, broken timbers.

Billy dismounted and wandered into the devastated landscape that had once been his home. The inky shadows of bare, crooked trees fell between him and the rising moon. As he approached what should have been his father's inn, sparse, jagged members jutted up into his view like the shattered bones of some long-dead beast. Still in shock, Billy reached out to touch them. Only feeling the pitch under his fingers convinced him that he was not having a nightmare.

"Billy!" a voice whispered from behind.

Billy spun around. "What?"

Again the voice whispered. "Billy."

Billy scanned the shadows of a large oak, which stood next to the remains of the barn. The great old tree had been Billy's friend. Without complaint, his coarse wooden limbs had generously held him up while climbing and spying, and protected him from the sun and rain. Now the old fellow's knobby arms were gone, reducing him to a thick, rough pillar.

Suddenly, a dark figure stepped out from within the tree. Billy jumped, thinking it some evil spirit or even the Night Queen bent on stealing his soul. Then just as sudden, the shadowy form took on familiar features.

"Nathan!" Billy said, relieved to be talking to the living.

Billy's boyhood friend and tormentor stepped forward again. "Aye, it's me. I knew ya would show up sooner or later."

"Ya did?"

"Aye. It's been a few days—"

"Where's my father?"

"At my house."

"Is he hurt?"

Nathan's face became grim. His eyes wandered as he kicked at the sooty foot of the oak.

"What is it?"

"He is an old man, and—"

"Let's go!" Billy ran to Briallen.

"Wait!"

"I'm sorry, old girl." Billy mounted Briallen. "We gotta run just a little more tonight before we can rest."

Briallen stepped into a trot in the direction of the village. Billy's mind was on nothing but his father.

Nathan ran up behind them. "Wait!"

Billy stopped and reached a hand down to him. "Climb on. Briallen can take us both."

Nathan got up behind Billy and clung to his waist. He was now a large man and easily twice Billy's weight, but Briallen wasn't one to bellyache.

"Who taught ya to ride?" Nathan asked.

Without a thought for how dubious it sounded, Billy answered, "Prince Gaelyn."

Nathan opened his mouth to object but said nothing. Billy nudged Briallen into a canter, and Nathan decided to hold on and keep his mouth shut for the remainder of the ride. By the time they arrived at his home, Nathan was full of questions, but Billy hopped down from the horse and never gave him a chance.

Branedthwain, Nathan's pretty wife, opened the door before Billy took three steps. She held it open in amazement as he marched by her.

"Don't stand there with the door open!" her husband chided.

Branedthwain looked curiously at her husband, who was holding the reins of a strange lathered-up horse. "Where are you going?" she silently asked with her expression.

"I gotta tend to the horse," he said, gesturing to the back of the house. "I'll be in as soon as I'm through." He then turned and led Briallen to the barn.

Billy found his father asleep in the only real bed. His face was pale and puffy, with bruises and abrasions over much of it. There were bandages around his hands and chest. Billy pulled up the covers to tuck them around his father. Gently, he took John's hand to put it under the blanket.

Just then, John opened his eyes. "William," he whispered.

Billy looked into John's face. One eye was swollen shut, but the other was clear and focused. "Father, you should be asleep."

"Ya shouldn't have come back," John said, before starting to cough.

Billy helped his father roll over on his side to make the coughing easier. As John lay back on the pillow, Billy saw a trace of blood on his lips. He grabbed a nearby bandage and wiped them clean.

John's voice was hoarse. "Ya must leave, William."

"Not without you, Father."

John's one good eye glanced around the room, and Billy followed it. There wasn't much to the little house: a kitchen, table, chairs, a few odds and ends, and Branedthwain, of course, who stood idly by in the kitchen. Then Billy noticed two very young children asleep in the corner, near the hearth, and remembered that Nathan was now a father. He smiled gratefully to Branedthwain, then returned his attention to his father.

John motioned for Billy to come closer. "Is Nathan in the house?"

"No. Why?"

"I don't want him to hear what I'm about to tell ya."

Billy looked again over his shoulder at his hostess. He had known Branedthwain since they were children. She had always been deaf and mute, but she communicated so well that hardly anyone noticed.

"What is it, Father?"

John took Billy's hand. "William, I'm dyin'—"

"No, Father!"

"Yes, William. It's high time ya knew the truth. I thought keepin' it a secret would protect ya, but now I know that it wouldn't have mattered."

"What do ya mean?"

"You have a destiny, William."

"I know, Father. I've come to understand that, in part, but can you tell me what it is?"

John smiled weakly. "I wish I could. You're gonna have to figure that one out yourself."

"Yes, Father."

"The ring ... It was your mother's, and is a part of your destiny. It will help you find your way."

Billy held up his hand and examined the ring. In the dim light, the simple gold band shone with its usual warm glow.

"Ya wear it on your hand?" his father said.

"We've come to an agreement of sorts."

John nodded. "I understand. William ... I am not your father."

"You are the only father I've truly known."

John's eyes narrowed. "You're not surprised? Ya knew already then?"

"Only recently." There was sadness in Billy's voice.

"William, have ya discovered your true identity?"

Billy sighed. "I am the son of Queen Eleanor."

John's eyes widened. "Then your father ... King William?"

"Aye." Billy looked at the floor. "I just don't understand how—"

"Sir Sedgemore."

"Sir Sedgemore?"

"Aye, it's all in his journal."

"His journal?"

"Aye. If you read it, you may not like what ya find. I added some to it myself and then hid it in—"

"Wait, Father." Billy held up his hand. Slowly Billy reached over and touched John. As he desired, there was a flash of bright light, and he entered the realm of his father's memories.

John's mind was like no other Billy had touched. Feelings of warmth and hospitality permeated him. When Billy's vision had cleared, he found himself outside The Valley's Finest Inn, only not the same inn he remembered. It was evening, and John—looking much younger than Billy could ever remember—was collecting firewood. An old tan hound accompanied him.

"There's a lad." John patted the dog's head. "What a sunset, 'ey Rascal?"

Billy watched as the story of his life with John was revealed. He witnessed the joys and the struggles, the laughter and the tears, and through it all he felt the love that his father had so freely given to him.

Billy looked his father in the face and touched his chest. "I always wondered how you got that scar."

John smiled. "The price of fatherhood ... my prince."

"Father ... I love you."

"I love you too, my son. Now ya must go. The man who did this to me might be back at any moment."

"Who was it, Father?"

"An old acquaintance," John wheezed.

Billy pulled the covers up around his father. "Was it the same man what burned down the inn the first time?"

"Aye, Sygeon they called him." John's eyes widened. "The *first* time?" He tried to sit up. "The inn! The inn!"

Billy gently held him down to the bed. It amazed him how easy it was. It tightened Billy's guts to see his father so weak. "Ya mustn't move, Father. There isn't anything that can be done now. You must rest."

Billy's words struck a chord, and John relaxed into his pillow. "I'm very tired, William."

"I know, Father." Billy tucked the covers in around John.

"So very tired."

"Rest."

Billy kept vigil over John, but eventually he succumbed to exhaustion and fell asleep, hunched over, with his hand on his father's. He slept without dreaming, then suddenly sat up, as if someone had called his name.

It was a few hours before dawn, but the man Billy knew as Father had passed away in the wee hours and would never see the sun rise. Billy clutched John's hand and held it to his breast. He shook his father, desperately hoping that he was only in a deep sleep.

"Father," Billy pleaded tearfully, "wake up!" But John did not stir. "Father ... I still need you."

In his despair, Billy was struck by an idea. He concentrated on his father and then placed his right hand over his father's heart. "Come back to me!" he pleaded. "Live!"

All at once his mother's ring became hot as fire itself. Billy cried out in agony as it burned into his flesh, but it was too hot for him to even remove. All he could do was hold it out and endure the excruciating pain. Then the heat subsided, and Billy was left with the pain of his heart—an ache that made the discomfort in his hand unimportant.

Nathan immediately came to Billy's side. His boyhood companion had thrown himself across the still, lifeless form of his father. The boy wept, his body shaking with each sob. Nathan quietly turned around and went to calm his children, who had been frightened by Billy's outburst.

* * *

Nathan and Billy buried John beside his wife and their infant son, on the hill overlooking what had been the valley's finest inn. It had taken some convincing, but Nathan finally agreed to perform the burial before dawn.

Sunlight crept into the Valley of the Yew, peeling back the low-hanging fog, like a comforter on the earth's bed. The two men watched in reverent silence as the sun restored the valley's colors. Then Billy hoisted himself into Briallen's saddle and secured the oilskin satchel containing Sir Sedgemore's journal.

"Why do ya have to leave, Billy? Maybe you could rebuild the inn, like your father."

Billy looked at the man who as a boy had harried and bullied him. "You've a beautiful family, Nathan."

"Thank you."

"You must all forget that ya even saw me, or you could lose everything ya hold dear."

"What's goin' on, Billy? Who are ya runnin' from?"

"The men who killed my father ... and they will be back! For your own safety, ya must know nothin' of me."

"Billy ... Fare ye well."

"Thank you for everythin', Nathan. I can never repay ya."

"Aw, just consider it payback, for all the rotten things I done to ya when we was young."

Billy smiled. "You're a fine man, Nathan. I hope someday to see ya again."

Billy nudged Briallen, and she carried him into the woods. As he disappeared over the hill, he called back, "Nathan! Forget!"

As Billy made his way from the Valley of the Yew, the trees, rocks, and animals, including the horse beneath him, were as distant as the stars. He was bound in his body—a silent witness. Nothing touched him. He felt utterly alone.

CHAPTER TWENTY-SEVEN

The Night Queen

Billy had hidden in the trees all afternoon and evening, watching merchants in wagons, messengers, soldiers, and various riders pass by. Judging from the traffic, something big was about to happen, but for now the King's Road was graveyard quiet.

He had, thus far, managed to avoid the well-traveled road, but the gorge ahead would take two or more days to ride around. Crossing the bridge would only take a few minutes. As soon as he was across, he would head back into the forest, cut across the rugged hill-country to Dyven, and hop a ship to Erin. It was only a small stretch of road to cover—perhaps a half mile including the bridge—but there were no clouds in the sky, and the moon shown down on the road, clearly illuminating any who dared set foot on it.

Billy cautiously touched the dust of the King's Road with his toe, testing it like water. It seemed safe enough, so he stepped on to it with both feet. His mother's ring had tingled all day, and now it squeezed his finger fretfully.

"If I don't go now, I may never make it," he told the ring.

He scanned right and left before leading Briallen from the brush. Then, thoroughly convinced he had the road to himself, he climbed on the loyal mare and urged her toward the bridge.

The soft thud of Briallen's hooves cut through the eerie silence of the moonlit road as Billy eyed the shadowy trees on either side. Without warning, the sound of her clomping hooves was echoed behind them.

Billy spun round in the saddle and scanned the road to their rear. Shadows melted, and moonlight birthed a pale horse, breathing steam and staring with eyes of flame. The shadows clung to the beast: first smokelike, then liquid, then forged by moonbeams into immutable, unyielding steel. Once fully hammered into substance by the light, Billy saw that she that sat upon the horse was the black-clad, owl-faced Night Queen.

Billy dug his heels into Briallen. "Hyah!"

The prince's faithful mount leapt into a gallop, churning up chunks of road into the air. Billy glanced over his shoulder, and his heart leapt to his throat. The Night Queen was close behind and gaining. Again he spurred Briallen on, but alas the valiant mare was no match for the unearthly beast behind her.

The road turned, and the bridge came into view. Billy was instantly feverish, his mind burning with desperation. There was nothing for him to do but go forward and pray for some miracle to deliver him.

Briallen's hooves slammed down on the first oaken planks of the bridge and shattered the silence of the gorge with thunder. A breath later, the noise was doubled by their pursuer. The rumble became deafening as they neared the middle of the bridge.

Billy stole a look over the side and glimpsed a tiny silver river winding through the distant gorge bottom. He glanced up across the gorge and was surprised to see three riders coming up the road.

At first, the riders moved slowly, appearing to be simple, weary travelers, but as Billy crossed the middle of the bridge, they picked up their pace, and he could see they rode their mounts like noblemen. When they came into the open, his eye caught moonlight reflected off a shield and lance. With each step closer, they became more familiar, until he knew them for three knights of Orgulous: Sir Owein, Sir Darn, and Sir Gareth.

Billy called out to them. An instant later he realized they were undoubtedly hunting him. However, he believed their treatment of him would have to beat whatever the Night Queen had in mind, so he called out again. "Owein!"

"Billy!"

Billy looked again over his shoulder. The Night Queen was nearly upon him. He could see her violet, gemlike eyes glaring at him through the owl's visage of her helm. Her mount snorted steam at Briallen's hindquarter. She leveled her spear at Billy and continued to gain inches on him until he could count the cruel iron barbs on its tip.

Suddenly, a new thunder echoed from the bridge. Billy looked ahead and saw Sir Owein charging towards him with his lance lowered into position. Sir Gareth and Sir Darn were a few lengths behind.

Seeing the point of Owein's lance bearing down on him terrified Billy, but he knew he couldn't stop, or the Night Queen would surely skewer him. Billy drove Briallen onward, praying that Sir Owein might miss him. He shut his eyes against the coming blow and hugged Briallen's neck. The thunder of hooves on the bridge pounded Billy's ears. Owein was right on top of him.

Crash!

Splinters and sparks filled the air as Sir Owein and the Night Queen collided. Billy, realizing that he hadn't been struck, straightened and looked behind him.

Sir Owein lay half over the bridge railing—his body pinned to an upright by the Night Queen's lance. Although still mounted, she had been brought to a stop.

Billy dug into Briallen's sides and turned forward just in time to catch Sir Gareth's outstretched arm on the chin. Billy was wiped from the saddle and then somersaulted backwards over his mount's rear. The ground leapt up to strike him, knocking the wind from his lungs and continuing to beat him as he tumbled down the road like a half-filled barrel of wheat.

Briallen, true to her training, galloped a few yards and slowed to a trot before stopping.

Billy lay on his back. The starry sky spun while his lungs fought to draw breath. He clenched his eyes against the pain that abruptly reported from his entire body and rolled over on his side. Slowly, he pushed up from the dust, trying to force some air into his lungs, but it was like taking bones from a dog.

Suddenly, more thunder and the clash of steel rang from the bridge. Billy looked up to see Gareth and Darn fighting back the Night Queen, in an attempt to rescue the fallen Owein.

Sir Gareth crowded in next to his attacker, attempting to drive her back down the bridge, but she did not budge. She swung her long black sword over her head. Then a shower of sparks lit up the bridge as she sheared off the top of Gareth's shield with a single blow. She next beat down on Darn, cutting through his shield and into his arm. The knight cried out in pain but continued to fight.

The Night Queen's eyes sought out Billy as she slashed and parried with her opponents. She drove her horse forward, wedging herself between the knights and closer to Billy, but the knights would not let her pass. Flashes of light bounced off their armor and the bridge supports as she rained down blow after blow on the king's warriors.

At last, Sir Gareth got in a clean shot, which knocked off the Night Queen's helmet. Her head was swayed for a moment, but then she rose up with the fury of fire in her eyes. She glared at Gareth and shield-bashed his chin while he was still awestruck by her beautiful, alien features. Immediately she followed with a lunge at Darn whose wounded arm had become too weak to hold up his shield. Blood gushed from the man's abdomen as the black sword penetrated his armor.

Darn's sword dropped to the planks of the bridge with a clank. The Night Queen tugged on her sword, but it was caught fast in her victim's armor. The knight grasped the sword lodged in his innards. He rolled forward and fell into her. Again she struggled to retrieve her weapon.

At that moment, Gareth struck at her from behind. His sword found its mark between her backplate and pauldron. She wailed as blood streamed from her shoulder. Instantly, she wheeled around, swatting Gareth's sword aside and nearly knocking him off his mount. Then, while he was still off balance, she drew her dagger and pounced on him. She struck at his face repeatedly, but each time the valiant knight managed to knock aside her blows.

Billy finally felt the breath returning to his pained lungs, and he rose to his feet. He gave a short whistle, and Briallen came to him.

Now all the combatants and their mounts crowded up against the side of the bridge. Gareth, arched backwards off the side of his horse, was barely able to maintain his seat and fend off the vicious attacks of the furious Night Queen. Darn feebly grabbed at her leg while his horse continued to drive them against the side. A loud creak came from the bridge as their weight came against the railing.

Both Gareth and the Night Queen hesitated, and then Gareth punched his opponent. Her face was flung back, but immediately returned, bloody and more enraged than before. She slashed feverishly at Gareth, cutting into his arm and once across his cheek.

Gareth grabbed the wrist of her dagger hand and her throat. The Night Queen responded by clawing at his eyes with her free hand, before reciprocating the chokehold he had on her. Neither one had a clear advantage.

Billy mounted Briallen and started to ride away from the bridge. He got only a few steps before he stopped to look back. The Night Queen glared up at him with all the venom she could muster.

Gareth gasped for air. He tried to say something but only sputtered.

Billy turned Briallen around and headed for the bridge. The personal danger didn't matter to him, nor did the knights' obligation to take him back for execution. He only knew that he couldn't leave them to the mercy of the Night Queen.

As Billy approached, both the Night Queen and Gareth looked up at him. Gareth summoned up his strength and said in a raspy voice, "Get out of here, Billy."

The Night Queen struck him in the throat and started toward Billy, but Gareth would not let go. She hissed at him and renewed her attack.

Just then, Owein managed to wrench the Night Queen's spear from his body. He turned the grisly, barbed weapon and drove it into her back with both hands.

Sparks flew, and a shrill screech burst from the Night Queen's mouth as she threw her arms open wide. Owein held on to the spear and was thrust backwards. Simultaneously, Darn's mount nudged the others, and they all swayed against the side of the bridge.

Snap! The heavy railing shattered, twisting the nearest support with a crunch. The bridge groaned, and the occupied section dropped abruptly to one side. The combatants scrambled to climb over each other and escape, but the sudden tilt and the momentum of the horses carried them further into the gap.

Billy dismounted and stepped on to the collapsing bridge. The horses whinnied and danced on the pitching, groaning planks, sending shock waves through the wood under his feet.

The Night Queen freed herself from her spear as Gareth's wide-eyed horse skidded out from under him and fell into the gorge. Despite her wounds and Gareth's weight, she clawed her way over Darn and his mount, never taking her eyes off Billy.

The planking beneath them sagged further, and Billy fell on his backside. He grabbed for a bridge support but missed and slid down toward the panicked horses. The Night Queen dragged Darn's body from his saddle. The knight fell between the frantic, slipping hooves of the horses with a metallic clash and shooshed over the edge into the gorge.

Billy backpedaled as fast as he could, trying to stay out of the tangled mess of horses and warriors. In the blink of an eye, Darn's horse stomped Billy's ankle, and he cried out in pain.

The Night Queen grabbed hold of Darn's saddlebow and dragged herself forward. She was directly above Billy now, and she drew back her dagger to strike him. "You'll never see Tirn Aill!" she hissed.

Suddenly Owein appeared next to Gareth, and they grabbed the Night Queen by the arm and torso. The bridge twisted with a bang, and they all slid into the gap. The Night Queen screamed, "No!" and desperately reached for Billy as the knights and horses dragged her over the edge.

Billy slid toward the edge directly behind them. He saw the gorge bottom racing towards him and the edge of the bridge go by under his feet. Just then his shirt caught on a splintered plank, causing him and his heart to come to an abrupt stop. He dangled over the precipice in petrified silence. The only sound was the wind in the trees, then a loud crash echoed through the gorge, restarting his heart.

The bridge creaked, and Billy turned to grab hold of its boards. Once he had wedged his fingers between the planks, he tore himself free from the splintered wood and climbed up the bowed bridge. The structure swayed and bounced with each handhold or foothold, complaining almost as much as his injured ankle.

Finally, Billy stood on the rim of the gorge with Briallen. He looked down to where the Night Queen and King William's knights had met with their fate.

"Why did she say I would never see Tirn Aill? How did she know I'm headed there?"

He glanced once more into the gorge, which had nearly claimed him with the others. Its black depths drew him forward with an open invitation. Still shivering, he mounted Briallen and trotted from the King's Road into the trees.

CHAPTER TWENTY-EIGHT

Convergence

Billy entered Dyven under the cover of night. He left Briallen near the old abbey where he furtively purloined a small bag of oats for her. He crossed the orchard and climbed onto the wall where he had seen his first city street. Thanks to the ring, his injured ankle was now a minor annoyance. He scrutinized the dimly lit street, then plucked an apple and dropped to the cobblestones.

Billy picked his way through the winding alleys of the city, looking for the spot where he first met Stitch. Along the way, he *borrowed* some clothes, which were conveniently left out for him by some generous laundress. They were nearly as ragged as the clothes given him by Gryff—which he left in exchange—but they were clean, and so he left a silver coin for her trouble.

Billy wandered for an hour, until he finally stumbled across the little shop with the shoe over the door. Billy sat down behind some barrels, pulled his new cloak around him, and waited for the dawn.

At last, the sound of peddler songs began to rise throughout the city. Billy stayed put, hoping that Stitch would show up soon. Suddenly, he was dragged from behind the barrels into the alley.

"What are ya doin' here?" Stitch asked, clutching Billy's cloak front.

"Stitch! It's me! Billy!"

"I knowed it was you," Stitch snarled. "Now what're ya doin' here?"

"Lookin' for you."

"Now ain't that nice. You're lookin' for me! The whole bloomin' country's lookin' for you!"

"I know."

"Lucky for me that I found ya, first."

"Lucky for you?"

"Aye," Stitch said. "You're my out."

"Your out?"

"Don't act so stupid!" Stitch shoved Billy against the wall of the alley. "When I turn ya in, I'll get me a reward that'll set me up for good."

"I thought you would help me."

"Help you?" Stitch was on the verge of laughing. "Why should I help a lyin', murderin' thief like you?"

"I didn't do it, Stitch!"

Stitch stared keenly into Billy's eyes. "I must be the king of all fools," he said before releasing Billy.

"Why? Because you believe me?"

"No," the hardened street urchin grumbled. "Because I should still turn ya in!"

"But ya won't?"

"Naw."

Billy smiled at Stitch. "Now, here's what I need—"

"Whoa there!" the boy said, holding up his hands. He took a moment and looked both ways down the alley. "I haven't said I'd help ya."

Billy looked Stitch square in the face and without pleading asked, "Will you?"

The good-hearted thief threw up his hands and shrugged. "Why not? They'll probably hang me anyway. Might as well be for somethin' I did."

Billy put his hand on Stitch's shoulder. "I hope it won't come to that. I only need your help long enough to get out of town."

"Then leave now! Just steal a horse or—"

"I have to get to Erin."

"The Emerald Isle?" Stitch screwed up his face.

"Aye."

"It gets stranger and stranger."

"What?"

"There happens to be two Albion ships in port right now. They're both sailin' to Erin—one today—the other in a few days."

"Great! What's so strange about that?"

"Ships from Albion hardly ever come here this time of year. An' no one wants to go to Erin, what with Gwythia about to attack any moment. An' then you come, lookin' for a ship to Erin ... It's strange."

"Lucky."

"Ya make your own luck. This is strange."

"What are the ships' named?"

"One is the Windan, the other ... the Mean Gold, or some such."

Billy nodded. "How do I get to the ships?"

Stitch pointed up the alley. "Go past the market, then follow your nose."

"But I can't just stroll over there! What if I'm seen?"

Stitch wrinkled his nose and scratched his head. "There is a way ... but I'll have to show ya."

"And I won't be seen?"

"I don't know," Stitch said. "I spotted ya behind those barrels easy enough. Were ya tryin' to hide?"

Billy remained silent.

"Well, ya better stick close to me, and do exactly as I say!"

"Fine."

* * *

Stitch took Billy down many narrow alleys and across a few rooftops. They avoided contact with people except where they had no choice. They even waited in the refuse of a gutter, as guardsmen passed over them.

By noon they were atop a large warehouse near the docks. Billy's own wretched smell overwhelmed him. He hadn't any idea how anyone could follow his nose under such conditions, until he got a whiff of the docks. Billy mentally went over the convoluted path they had taken, trying to memorize it. It seemed impossible, and if he had to do it *at night...*

Stitch pointed to two ships, each with two tall masts, floating amid the fishing boats. "That's them."

At that moment there were only two men on deck. The first was a big, hairy man with a beard, who reminded Billy of Sir Aonghas. He shouted at the other man and pointed, with his only hand, to the stern of the ship. The second man, who was even larger than the first, nodded curtly and obediently ran to the back. Billy's attention stayed with the one-armed man.

"That must be the captain," Stitch said.

"Ya think so?"

Stitch laughed. "If not, that giant would squash him like a bug."

"Giant?" Billy whispered, taking another look at the hulking sailor.

"Ya ever seen a giant before?"

"Only once."

Billy watched the captain as he walked to the bow. He stopped at the railing and whistled to two women who waved at him from across the docks. On the side, beneath his feet, painted in red letters was the name of the ship.

Billy read the name aloud. "The *Gyldan Mene.*"

"That's the name," Stitch affirmed. Then he looked at Billy with an expression of surprise on his face. "Ya know that ship?"

"No. I read the name on her side."

Stitch's expression changed from surprise to amazement. "You can read?"

"Aye."

"Come on," Stitch said, crawling to the back of the warehouse. "Let's get a better look."

Billy followed Stitch down a rope at the side of the building into a maze of crates and barrels. As they made their way to the front of the warehouse, Billy contemplated how much Stitch knew and did, all without the ability to read or write. The little thief, like most everyone, did fine despite an ignorance of letters and the like.

Stitch stopped at the mouth of the alley and assessed the docks. At last he stood up and waved for Billy to follow. Billy studied the area and donned the hood Stitch had provided, before exiting.

It felt great to walk on the docks, in the sunshine, mingling amongst housewives, servants, sailors, and fishmongers. Gulls called overhead, while below children joyfully screamed with the excitement of playing in the water. In those strange, carefree, and happy surroundings, Billy almost forgot that he was a fugitive. As he approached the *Gyldan Mene*, he wished that he could forget—for just one afternoon.

The peace was abruptly pierced by a loud, tenor voice shouting, "Stop those boys!"

Billy spun around and found himself in the middle of a widening path that split the crowd like wind in a wheat field. Stitch had vanished, leaving Billy standing completely alone. At the far end of the clearing there were six guardsmen. Situated amid their spear tips was a slovenly dressed fat man on a shaggy black cob. The man made eye contact with Billy and leered like a snake with a mouse in its den.

"Derian," Billy muttered.

"Take him!" Derian barked to his men.

Instantly the guards lowered their weapons and charged. Without thinking, Billy ran in the opposite direction. Fortunately, the crowd had also split behind him; unfortunately, the only place for Billy to run was farther down the pier, and beyond that ... the bay.

Billy recognized his limited situation as the end of the pier drew near. He looked over his shoulder and saw the guards hot on his tail. *If only there was somewhere to run. I could lose these old men.* His mind raced as his feet diminished the possibilities. Suddenly he was at the end of the pier. Billy stopped.

The guardsmen slowed down to approach him cautiously. He shifted his focus, back and forth, between them and the drop to the water. The tide was out, making the water seem far away.

"Give it up, boy."

"Aye, the sergeant's right."

"Ya got nowhere to go."

Billy backed up until his heels were on the edge of the pier. He grabbed a post to steady himself.

The sergeant stepped in front of his men. "I can see what you're thinkin', boy ... but there be sharks in them waters."

Billy carefully eyed the water.

"You don't know how to swim ... do ya, boy?"

Billy smiled at the sergeant. "As a matter of fact, I do."

With that, Billy stepped back and dropped from sight. The guards rushed forward to witness him plunge into the chilly waters of the bay.

As they scratched their heads and watched Billy's bubbles rise to the surface, one of the dumbfounded guards said, "He did it."

"Aye," the guard next to him said. "I wouldn't have done it."

The sergeant nudged his companion. "That's because ya haven't got any guts, Dairn."

"Well, we'll see how much guts he's got when the sharks finish with him!" the man said defensively.

The guard who had remained quiet to this point spoke up. "There aren't any sharks in there."

"There aren't?" Dairn exclaimed.

The sergeant grinned. "Naw. I just said that to keep him from jumpin'."

"Oh," Dairn said. "How long is he gonna be down there, anyway?"

As if to answer Dairn's query, Billy came up, gasping for air. He looked up at the guards standing on the dock far over his head.

"Stay there, boy," their sergeant shouted. "We'll throw ya down a rope."

"No thanks!" Billy said, then turned and swam away.

"You'll drown!"

Dairn cupped his hands to shout at Billy. "The sharks will eat ya if ya don't come out right now!"

Billy paid the guards and their sergeant no heed. He just concentrated on swimming for the opposite shore. It would be a long swim, but he didn't have any choice.

When Billy had swum about fifty yards, he looked back over his shoulder. The guardsmen were still standing at the end of the pier and arguing with Derian, who had ridden out to them.

"Go after him, ya fools!" the corpulent man demanded from his horse.

"I can't swim," the sergeant stated.

"Neither can I," another said.

"Nor I," Dairn confessed.

Shortly, all six guards were engrossed in a discussion of why none of them had ever learned to swim, and how many of their relatives didn't know how to either, and wasn't it funny that they should all happen to grow up inland and end up on the same squad together, and yet they never knew—

"Shut up!" Derian screamed at the top of his lungs. "Shut up, shut up, shut up!"

The guards quieted and stood at attention.

Derian leaned forward in the saddle. "I suppose none of ya knows how to use a boat either."

Each man looked to the left and right, expecting one of the others to say that he knew how to use a boat.

"My cousin's brother-in-law had a boat," Dairn offered.

The other five guardsmen exploded with laughter. Dairn gawked at them perplexed, but then fell victim to their contagious guffaws.

Derian scowled at the bay as his prey continued to swim away. "This isn't over, Billy," he muttered.

Derian slowly turned his horse and rode back towards the city. He left the squad assigned to him ridiculously rolling on the planks of the pier, holding their middles in uncontrollable, belly-laughing pain.

* * *

Late the next day, Sir Hugh arrived at Cyndyn Hall. Eadwig, the chamberlain, greeted him in the courtyard and instructed the stable boy to tend to his mount.

"Careful when you give him a rubdown, Thomas," Hugh cautioned. "Splendore likes his mane brushed, but if you get too many tangles he'll bite. Of course, you're already acquainted."

The boy smiled knowingly and bowed to Hugh, then warily eyed the steed. He tugged on the reins, but Splendore Pomponnel would not budge. Hugh patted the horse on the side and clicked his tongue, at which time Splendore allowed the boy to take him away.

"That's a very stubborn and spirited animal," Eadwig said.

Hugh nodded. "Aye. He's a Cyndyn."

Eadwig gave Hugh a shocked expression and Hugh laughed. Slowly, the old caretaker's lips curved upward, and he snickered.

"Aye," Eadwig said knowingly. "That he is."

"Who is what?" Lady Myrredith asked from behind them.

Hugh turned to face her. Myrredith was completely clad in black. Her beautiful red hair flowed loosely about her shoulders. Hugh's hand impulsively reached for her, before he constrained it. "Milady," he said bowing properly.

Lady Myrredith unexpectedly reached out and hugged him. "Hugh," she said softly, "how good it is to see you."

"And you," he answered.

Myrredith turned and led Hugh into Cyndyn Hall. Eadwig followed at a discreet distance.

"You do know about Kathryn?" Hugh asked cautiously.

"Aye," she answered curtly. "I still feel ...."

Myrredith painfully searched for the right words. In the end, she only shook her head.

"I know," Hugh said. "And Billy—"

"Hugh!" Myrredith whispered, barely able to contain her excitement.

"What is it?" Hugh asked curiously.

"I have a secret I would share with you."

Hugh scanned the courtyard. From atop the steps he could see that it was empty—aside from Eadwig and themselves. "What is it?"

"Not here," she said, continuing into the great hall. "I'll allow you to freshen up. Have something to eat, then we can talk."

Hugh knit his eyebrows. "As you wish."

Hugh hastily cleaned the road dust from his body and changed clothes. Then just as quickly, he devoured half a plate of food and asked where he might find his hostess. He was directed to her garden and went there post-haste.

Lady Myrredith was strolling alone in her garden when Hugh arrived. He watched her as she sampled the fragrance of a rose.

Myrredith spotted her admirer. "That was quick."

"Well," Hugh said, with a weighty sigh, "I have much to tell you."

"Allow me to tell you my news first. What I have to say may lift your burden."

"Yes, tell me," Hugh said, feeling her excitement.

Myrredith waited until Hugh was next to her before she spoke. "William is safe," she said with a smile.

"Yes, otherwise the countryside wouldn't be crawling with men searching for him. I can't believe how many bounty hunters I saw today!"

"Aye. Even Owein, Gareth and Darn have been through Dyven ... but they won't catch William!"

Hugh's expression became very serious. "Myrredith ... do you know where Billy is?"

"Not exactly."

"What do you mean *not exactly?*"

"Not exactly!"

Hugh looked into her eyes. He gently placed a hand on her shoulder. "Tell me what you know."

Myrredith first related how Billy left her the note on the road—much to Hugh's amazement. Then she told him that Billy had been sighted in Dyven the day before.

"Yesterday?" The King's Champion tensed. His eyes shifted from side to side, as if he were figuring something. "Then he's here."

"Or was," Myrredith added. Then she became concerned with Hugh's behavior. "Say, what is it, Hugh?"

"*Was?*"

"Well … a ship left Dyven yesterday, headed for Erin. Rumor has it, William was aboard."

"No." Hugh turned away.

Myrredith took his hand and turned him around. "What is it, Hugh? What aren't you telling me?"

"I—" Hugh's breath caught in his lungs. He closed his eyes and exhaled. "I must bring him back."

"What?"

"To Orgulous." Hugh turned away again.

"Hugh!"

"It is my duty."

"Your duty? To betray your friend?"

"I am the King's Champion!" Hugh snapped.

"William is your friend!"

"I must do as my king bids me."

"But William didn't do it!"

"The king himself pronounced him guilty."

"The king is not always right."

"But he is always the king!" Hugh took a deep breath. "And until he isn't, I must obey."

"You know William didn't do it."

"Aye, but what I think doesn't matter."

"Doesn't it?" Myrredith said, trying to reason with him.

Hugh's shoulders sank. "No."

"Ooh!" Myrredith clinched her fists and pursed her lips. "Do you think that performing this duty will restore your father's name or bring back your mother?"

"No!" Hugh shouted. "I can't bring her back, or even make up for all the years Ergyfel stole from her, but I can restore my father's good name."

"How? How will William's death do that?"

"When I bring Billy back, it will clear my father's name," Hugh said. "*And* clear you and me of all charges."

The proud Lady of Cyndyn Hall stomped the ground. "No! I will not allow you to clear my name with William's blood!"

"But you're not listening—"

"If you're doing this-this thing for *me*, then don't!"

"I have no choice."

"Your precious duty will cost William his life!"

"I will clear Billy as well! I promise."

Myrredith stared at Hugh and shook her head. "It will cost you your soul!"

"And what if I don't do it? Huh? Could you live anywhere else but here?"

"What do you mean, Hugh?"

"Could you run away with me, and leave all this behind?" Hugh gestured to the surrounding castle. "Could you leave your lands, your people, your home ... for a man who had forgotten his honor?"

"I can't just leave. My duty won't—" Myrredith fell silent. Finally she spoke again. "I guess we both have our duties."

"Then you understand."

"No. Not this. This *bloody* task of yours is wrong. Hugh, it will destroy you. It will destroy *us!*"

Hugh turned to Myrredith but, from shame, could not bring his eyes upon her. He gazed instead at the ground between his feet. "Myrredith ..." He wanted to tell her that he loved her, he needed her, and without her his life was meaningless.

"Leave, Hugh," Myrredith whispered. "Just leave."

Hugh took a step to walk away from the only woman he would ever love. He halted after the first step, struggling for the right words to say. All his instincts told him that leaving was wrong, but his conscience told him he must go. He took another difficult step away, then another. Just then he heard her voice and he froze.

"If you do this thing," she said shakily, "I don't ... I don't want to see you again."

In that instant, something twisted inside Hugh. He felt sure he was damned. By sheer will, he forced himself to leave the garden. A strange coldness crept into him and nested in his stomach. It was as if his soul had forsaken his body, and he was—beyond his comprehension—dead.

* * *

The Blood and Slobber Inn bustled that night. Many of the usual customers were present. The jokes were flowing in proportion to the ale, and for a change, the tavern was only living up to the last half of its name— albeit that might be corrected at any moment.

In a dark corner, Hugh sat brooding over his third tankard of mead. The hood of his traveling cloak, which he wore despite the warm environment, concealed his face in shadow. A full plate of food waited on the table in front of him, unchanged from when it arrived there, except that it was now cold as riverbed stones.

The buxom barmaid stood over him. "What's the matter, love? Not hungry? Food not to your likin', 'eh? Not that I blame ya. I wouldn't eat here myself if I didn't have to. Shall I take it away then? Ya don't talk much, do ya?"

The girl leaned over to pick up the plate, deliberately giving Hugh a good view of her "God-given talents." As she straightened and placed the plate on her tray, she saw that her performance had produced no reaction, at least not any of the reactions she was used to. Again she leaned forward, on the pretext of looking into his tankard.

"Uh-oh, almost out," she said, moving in close, but again the preoccupied knight disappointed her. She stood beside Hugh, closer than what was proper for two strangers, and waited.

"Is there anythin' I can *give* ya?" she asked pointedly.

At last the promiscuous girl relented. She leaned over once more, this time placing her face before his. She remained there, observing his handsome face and fervent eyes until he focused on her.

"How 'bout another mead?" she said with a kind smile.

Hugh gravely nodded. She started to leave, then stopped and turned back. "Oh, and my name's Heather, just in case ya change your mind."

At that moment, the fight that had been brewing across the room came to a head and Heather scurried behind the bar. Hugh glanced up with mild interest, then returned to his brooding. The scuffle quickly grew into a brawl that enveloped the far half of the tavern. It was turning into another fat-lipped-black-eyed-teeth-on-the-floor night at the Blood and Slobber. Suddenly, a pewter bowl flew across the room and smashed Hugh's nearly empty tankard. Mead poured through the slats of the wooden table onto his legs.

At the center of the cold void within Hugh, a spark ignited and instantly grew to fill the emptiness with white-hot fire. Hugh stood up and marched across the room.

He walked in-between the first two brawlers he came to and punched both of them at once. The men flew back with the force of his blows and lay on the floor. The next two had their heads cracked together. The fifth unfortunate oaf received a swift kick, and the sixth a vicious elbow. Hugh cut a broad swath through the melee, leaving a trail of battered, less quarrelsome men in his wake.

When the King's Champion reached the two scrappers who had started the free-for-all, they were embroiled in an eye-gouging, finger-biting wrestling match. All the others, having witnessed Hugh's approach, had stopped fighting and were waiting to see what he would do next. He grabbed the first man by his collar and the seat of his pants and tossed him over a table like a bucket of slops. Then he picked up the other man by the shirtfront and plopped him down in a chair. The dazed man stared at him.

Hugh got close to the sitting man's face. "I came in here to have a few quiet drinks ... and by God, I'm going to."

The man remained slack jawed while Hugh spoke, but when the knight turned to go back to his table, the man stood and grabbed a heavy soup bowl to brain him. Before he could bring it down on Hugh's head, Hugh spun and caught the man's wrist. Then Hugh hauled back and slammed him with a haymaker that jarred the teeth of everyone in the tavern. The man fell back into the chair and oozed onto the floor.

Hugh grunted, then turned and walked through the silent crowd to his table. Heather rushed over with a new tankard of mead.

"This one's on the house," she said with a smile and a curtsy.

Hugh nodded to her and started to take a drink. Before he tasted the mead, he looked around the room of people, who were still standing in awe of him. No one dared to say a word.

The door opened, and two men stumbled inside. One boisterously blathered over his friend's guffaws, "An' that's when she says to me, get yer dirty paws off of ..."

The two rosy-nosed men stopped abruptly when they perceived the silence surrounding them. They scanned the room nervously and then darted out the door for the street. Immediately, the tavern exploded with laughter. Before long, it returned to what Hugh took to be normal.

Sometime later, Hugh found himself still sitting at the same table, alone. He had lost count of the tankards of mead he swallowed, but still he couldn't escape his dilemma.

Hugh finished his drink. He looked up to catch Heather's eye and order one last tankard. His back stiffened and his eyes widened when they came across Don Miguel Medina Scarosa sitting across the table.

"So sorry, Sir Hugh," the Spaniard hissed. "I did no mean to startle you."

Hugh stared across at *the black peacock*. "So it is true."

Don Miguel looked curiously at the inebriated knight. "What is true?"

"Too much drink brings the devil to your table."

"No, no, no," Don Miguel said with a laugh. He tipped his head and gestured with his hands. "I will admit to having a silver tongue, a infinite wit, and devilish good looks, but no, I am no El Diablo."

Hugh laughed. Perhaps it was the alcohol, but for the first time he could remember, he actually found Scarosa humorous.

Don Miguel smiled back at him like a leopard. "That's much better, my most serious friend."

"I'll say!" Heather said from behind him.

Don Miguel twisted in his seat to look at the barmaid. His eyes caught sight of the voluptuous girl, and he grinned. "So, my beauty," he said, pouring on his usual syrupy charm, "you are familiar with my gloomy companion?"

She nodded. "He's the most sober drunk I think I've ever seen. No disrespect intended. Not that he can't ... throw up his heels."

"Throw up his heels?" Scarosa asked. "He did a dance for you?"

"No. Not exactly."

Hugh looked at the talkative barmaid with a raised eyebrow.

"Well," Heather said, "he's a natural-born bouncer, he is."

Don Miguel Scarosa roared with laughter. He pointed at Hugh and slapped the table.

"What is it?" Heather asked. "What's so funny?"

"Him!" Scarosa said between laughs. "A bouncer!"

"Why is that so funny?" Heather asked earnestly. "Who is he?"

Don Miguel stood and took Heather's hand. He fought to control his laughter. "Allow me introduce to you, Sir Hugh ... knight-errant, and Champion to King William."

Heather's jaw fell open, and Don Miguel erupted in another laughing fit. She stood motionless until Miguel closed her mouth with a finger under her chin. Heather lowered her eyes, curtsied, and promptly headed for the safety of the bar.

Hugh watched her bashfully disappear below the counter. "Strange!" he muttered. "She was more forward when she didn't know who I was."

Don Miguel seated himself and grinned at Hugh. "I think I know why you have come to Dyven."

Hugh returned his attention to the man sitting across from him. He crossed his arms and sat back in his chair. "Why?"

"You and me ... we are here for the same reason."

"I doubt it."

Scarosa smiled knowingly.

"Well ...?" Hugh prompted.

"Are you a betting man, Sir Hugh?"

"You know I'm not."

"Yes. Pity. I am a little ... How you say? Oh yes, a little short."

Hugh was losing patience with Don Miguel's meandering. "Get to the point!"

"Billy."

"What about him?"

"We are both here for him."

Hugh glared at the troubadour. "What do you want with Billy?"

"The reward of course! What else?"

"Reward?"

"Oh yes! There will be a great reward for the man who bring him in. Alive or dead."

Hugh lunged across the table and grabbed Scarosa by the throat, pulling him forward until their noses were almost touching. The tavern fell silent, and Hugh felt every eye upon him. A bead of sweat ran down the Spaniard's forehead and dripped onto the table.

"He will be alive," Hugh whispered.

"Of course," Miguel said.

Hugh pushed Scarosa back into his chair with disgust.

Don Miguel massaged his throat and swallowed as he stared dubiously at Hugh. "Alive. Yes, this is what I mean. I will give you half," he offered hoarsely, "if you take me with you."

"You can keep the filthy reward! I want nothing of it!"

Miguel grinned. "I was hoping you would say that."

"And I didn't say I would take you!" Hugh declared.

"I know. I know. But I have something you need."

"What could you have?"

"Information."

"Ha!" Hugh spat. "Gossip!"

Don Miguel stopped smiling. "No gossip. I know someone in this town. Someone who has—eh—special access."

"Who?"

"No-no-no." Miguel wagged a finger at Hugh. "If I tell you, then you will no need me."

Hugh was becoming more sober by the moment and wishing he weren't. "Very well, Scarosa."

"Then you will take me?"

"I will decide that once you've told me your information."

"But—"

"If it's good enough then I will *consider* your proposal."

"I have your word?"

"Miguel!"

"Yes. Very well. My source tell me that Billy was in town and—"

"I've heard that rumor too, Miguel! I thought you were going to tell me something substantial."

Scarosa raised his hand. "Please allow me finish. Prince Gaelyn horse—the one that show up missing the same time as Billy—well, it show up, here in town."

Hugh sat back in his chair and rubbed his chin. "And where is the horse now?"

"In the stable of the city guard. The captain take her to Cyndyn Hall tomorrow."

Hugh raised an eyebrow. "When did they find her?"

"A short while ago, but there is more if you are interested."

"Go on."

Scarosa leaned forward. "Billy has gone to Erin."

"Another rumor," Hugh said with a sigh.

"No. The boy that help him was finally captured and they question him."

"Captain Oswyn said he got away. Who questioned him?" Hugh demanded.

Miguel was quiet for a moment. He looked around suspiciously before answering. "Derian, the thief tracker."

Hugh pushed up from the table. "I want to question this boy myself."

"No."

"What do you mean, 'no'?"

"No possible. The boy, he meet with a ... accident."

Hugh glared at Scarosa disdainfully and sat. "What kind of *accident?*"

"Very unfortunate." The Spaniard shook his head. "He escape and was run down by a wagon."

For a long while, Hugh said nothing. He stared at the ceiling, contemplating Don Miguel's story and its veracity.

Again Scarosa asked, "Will you take me with you?"

Hugh looked him sternly in the eyes. "No."

"Why no?" Don Miguel complained. "My information is no good enough?"

"No, no. I just can't."

"What if I told you I still have something you need?"

Hugh rolled his eyes and sighed. "What now?"

"The *Gyldan Mene* leaves for Erin day after tomorrow."

"And?"

"And I have purchase the last two passages from her captain."

Hugh squinted at Scarosa. *If he has the only means to follow Billy at his disposal, then why didn't he say so from the first, instead of this long-winded foxhunt?*

"How much do you want for them?" Hugh asked.

"How much?" Scarosa placed his hand on his chest. "Sir Hugh, you hurt me to the fast. I only wish to share them with you."

"If you have all this information and the only means to follow Billy, then why do you want me along?"

"I am only a little man, Sir Hugh, but *you*, you are a warrior, a hero. We may need that to catch him. And who knows? Maybe there will be a song in it for you."

"No! There will be no songs about this cursed quest. And if I ever hear that you have writted one, then it is you whom I will be hunting."

"Fine. Have it your way." Scarosa smiled. "No songs. Does this mean you will take me?"

"I'm not sure who is taking whom," Hugh said, "but yes."

Miguel's smile broadened and he tapped Hugh's tankard with his goblet. "Good! You will no regret this."

Hugh glanced out the corner of his eye at the Spaniard. He inhaled to say that he already regretted it but remained silent. His mind moved on to the journey ahead. The feeling of inescapable damnation had returned, and with it, a fatalistic view towards the spiritual consequences of his choice—his duty. Hugh watched his new companion sip his wine and wondered if the sleazy troubadour had any concept of what he was getting himself into. *Who knows? Maybe musicians are just what they need in Hell!*

CHAPTER TWENTY-NINE

The Gyldan Mene

The night before the *Gyldan Mene* was to set sail, she anchored deep in Kelmyrr Bay. Oswyn, captain of Dyven's city guard, and the port authorities thought it a prudent move, considering recent dockside events and rumors. The ship's captain and his crew, having loaded their ship, were ashore enjoying a last night's frolic. As usual, Camion the giant was left behind to secure the ship.

There was only one problem with this logic: Camion, unlike everywhere else, had made a lady friend in this port, and he yearned to see her just one last time. He longed to look into her soft brown eyes and hear her gentle voice and perhaps stroke her long blonde hair or touch her soft pink skin. However, he was doggedly loyal to his captain, and as such he dared not leave his post. So, as with most sailors without their best girl, he sought comfort from Dionysus.

"But no!" the giant grumbled, lying on the deck. "Camion must stay with ship!" He took another long draught from the cask above his head and laid back. He allowed the wine to overflow his mouth and spill down his cheeks to the deck before he shut off the spigot.

Slowly, Camion talked and drank himself into oblivion. Therefore, no one saw the figure of a small man swim across the bay and quietly climb the anchor line onto the ship. Nor did anyone see this trespasser tiptoe over the sleeping giant and stow away into the cramped cargo hold.

* * *

The next morning, as the crew of the *Gyldan Mene* reluctantly returned from their night on the town, they were greeted by a grumpy giant who was only slightly less hung over than they. The captain brought several passengers aboard next, then showed his guests where to store their gear and gave the ship a quick once-over.

"No one came aboard last night, Camion?"

"No, Captain!"

"You are sure?"

"Camion stay here all night, Captain."

"Good, good," the captain said. "As soon as the rest of our passengers arrive, we'll get under way."

"Aye, Captain."

Shortly before high tide, the last two passengers of the *Gyldan Mene* came aboard. Both men were dressed in shabby dark cloaks and carried little in the way of gear. Despite their arrival on the same dinghy, they appeared to be strangers. The slighter of the two was a dark man who carried a lute and walked with a spring in his step. The other, while built larger and more athletic, plodded along. He kept his head covered and carried a small ragged bag and a child's coffin.

The crew protested when they saw the coffin, but the captain quickly put the "superstitious lot" in their place and welcomed the two men aboard. The captain then went to the stern, while the newcomers went to opposite sides of the ship and settled in.

The captain gave the word, and the anchor was raised. He barked several commands, and crewmen scurried up the rigging. Within a minute, the sails were deployed. The *Gyldan Mene* was under way. Within ten minutes she cleared the natural breakwater of Kelmyrr Bay and headed into the open sea.

Billy had never experienced the exhilarating feeling of a ship on the ocean. It was all so new, so exciting, so nauseating. He hadn't anticipated such a reaction, and it frightened him. At first he was afraid he would die, but after an hour he feared he wouldn't die soon enough. By far, his greatest fear was that his churning stomach might cause him to be discovered. It was all he could do to keep quiet each time he retched. After four hours of such torture, Billy was ready to turn himself in and take whatever horrible fate awaited him. *If the captain will just let me off the ship.* However, when he went to stand up, he found he didn't have the strength.

The darkness of the hold brightened as two sailors entered to collect supplies. "Good thing the sea's calm today," one said.

His companion nodded. "Aye. Some of the passengers look like farmers!"

"Aye, farmers!"

The two crewmen laughed and slapped each other on the back.

"Do ya think we should eat in front of them?" the first sailor asked as he crammed a trencher in his mouth.

"Only if ya offer them some. Common courtesy, ya know!"

The first mariner spat out the bread with a laugh. "Aye, but they won't take any."

"Well, that's more for us."

"If that storm catches up to us, we'll have all we can eat!"

The two sea dogs carried on, laughing at each other's jokes. They then exited, leaving Billy alone in the dark, fearful that the worst was yet to come.

Before nightfall, Billy's fears came to fruition. At first it was a subtle change, with a slight increase in the crash of waves against the bow. The water turned green, and the waves swelled, transforming the terrain of the sea into tall rolling hills. The ship surged upwards onto the hills only to drop off into the gullies between with a loud slap. The sky darkened, and thunder rumbled in the distance. Howling winds from the northeast buffeted the sails, causing the captain to send his men aloft to trim them.

Inside the hold, the air was unbearably oppressive. Rain and seawater started to spill into the compartment through joints in the upper-deck planking. Billy was being beaten from the inside by his tangled guts, and from the outside by cargo that had broken free. He now had a painful lump on his head and wanted desperately to escape the confines of his deteriorating sanctuary.

There was a horrendous boom, which rattled the ship's timbers and Billy's nerves. At that same moment, he saw a flash of bright light through the leaky cracks over his head. Instantly he was on his feet, scrambling for the hatch. The lightning was so close that Billy thought it must have struck the ship. After the initial adrenal response, the idea that the ship might be on fire kept him moving.

Wind-driven rain and seawater pelted Billy, instantly soaking him as he opened the hatch. The crew combated the storm while the passengers huddled together on the deck. Some prayed for salvation while others cried out in fear. Only two of the passengers looked untroubled by the storm. The first was a poor musician whose only interest was to protect his precious instrument. He fretted with a tattered lute cover, oblivious to his peril. The second man sat away from the others, calmly watching the sea. He held tightly to a small casket, which lay across his lap.

Billy cautiously crept out through the hatch and hid himself amongst some casks on deck. As he was settling in, a rogue wave bashed the ship and nearly sent him overboard. Billy quickly found a length of rope and lashed himself to the nearest cleat.

As he was getting back into his hiding place, Billy glanced over at the paying passengers. They wailed miserably, the pious and the ungodly alike.

The musician had lost, abandoned, or stored his lute somewhere out of sight.

The man with the child's coffin clung to it as if it held life instead of death. He still did not huddle with the others and daringly refused to hold on to anything but the sad little box. Oddly enough, this madman felt familiar to Billy. As if by design, a wave rolled over the deck and struck the man head-on. The water instantly receded, revealing Sir Hugh holding the diminutive casket.

Billy started to hail the King's Champion, but intuition stopped him. He looked at his hand; his mother's ring glowed dimly.

Billy fell back against the barrels, confused and shocked. Here was Sir Hugh—on the same boat—in disguise. Something was amiss. In a flash, the import of Billy's nightmares became clear.

"He's come after me," Billy muttered.

Hugh absently pulled the hood of his cloak back over his head. The wet, tattered cloth whipped wildly in the roaring tempest, while the inside of the noble knight was serene. He faced certain death at the hands of nature with no trepidation. He accepted this as just punishment for his sin. His blind, arrogant obedience to duty had brought him to this end.

Within the boundaries of the coldness that had invaded him at Cyndyn Hall, the terrible void still suckled on his essence. Hugh put down the little coffin and got to his feet, intending to let the next wave take him. At that moment the void changed. It was not empty after all, but filled with bitter heartbreak. The barrier burst, and sorrow poured into every corner of his being. Tears bled from his eyes and were instantly lost in the sea spray rolling down his face.

"I'm sorry, Father … Mother," he said to the wind. "I failed you."

The *Gyldan Mene* suddenly listed to the far side, forcing Hugh away from the edge. As the ship righted itself, he moved back to the railing and grabbed hold.

"Billy, my friend … forgive me. And Myrredith … I love you as no other, yet I allowed my pride to destroy what chance we might have had. I will regret that most of all, for eternity."

Hugh released the railing and waited for his wave.

Billy could see no tether around Hugh and became panicky when the King's Champion threw his arms wide in challenge to the sea.

Just then, Billy spotted the musician moving up behind Hugh. The man glanced around suspiciously, before putting his hands up and drawing back. It was clear to Billy that he meant to push the unsuspecting knight overboard.

Billy jumped out from his hiding place. "Hugh!"

Hugh gazed in the direction of the voice calling his name. Seeing Billy caused his legs to buckle momentarily, and he grabbed the rail to keep from falling. He was abruptly brought to his senses by the impact of a wave on one side and a man on the other.

The men fell, and the wave washed them to the center of the deck. Hugh sat up gaping at Billy. Without warning the musician kicked the King's Champion in the face, knocking him back to the planks. Then he drew a dagger and struck at his foe. Hugh recovered from the kick just in time to stop the descending blade. He elbowed his assailant and knocked the weapon from his hand.

The man fighting Sir Hugh miraculously stood and spun around to face him. There was another blade in his hand. Billy blinked out of disbelief. *That was the exact move the assassin used against Prince Gaelyn.* The man held out his hand for balance, and Billy saw the angry, red cross on his palm where Gaelyn had twice slashed him.

Billy hopped onto the barrel in front of him. "Assassin!" He then stepped forward, but reached the end of his tether, which threw him backwards to the deck.

As Billy regained his footing, he looked over the casks and saw the passengers attempting to disperse. Those fortunate enough to have a knife had cut their ties and were headed for the poop deck. The others desperately tried to free themselves. Sir Hugh was now on his feet, facing the assassin. He was still empty-handed.

The murderer thrust and slashed at Hugh. He circled around some gear on the deck and shortly found his tether hindering his movement. He grabbed the line to cut it with his knife. When he lowered the weapon, Hugh made his move and managed to get a hold on him. As the two combatants grappled, Billy struggled with the knot he had tied around his waist.

Hugh pushed his foe against the central mast and bent back his arm until he dropped the knife. Despite his strength and fighting experience, Hugh was hard pressed to keep hold of his wiry attacker. The man headbutted Hugh and slipped out of his grip. He grabbed the lantern hanging from the mast above him, then bashed Hugh in the side of the head. The King's Champion fell back, trying to shake off the stunning blow. His attacker struck again. This time, however, the lantern broke on Hugh's shoulder and spewed burning oil over the deck.

While Hugh rolled on the deck, attempting to snuff the fire on his arm and back, his assailant looked for his dropped knife. The ship, in its contest with the angry sea, pitched abruptly, tossing Hugh into a stack of cargo. A cascade of crates and barrels came crashing down on him. Several of the crates and one barrel shattered on impact, splattering their contents over the deck. The feeble flames of the broken lantern leapt across the planks, following a trail that led back to the broken barrel. In a flash, the fire spread, engulfing the crates and loose bundles.

The killer finally spotted his weapon and retrieved it. He then stepped towards the downed knight to finish him.

"Stop!" Billy shouted from behind the assassin.

The man froze and slowly turned. Lightning washed away the shadows from the murderer's face.

"Don Miguel," Billy muttered. "You're the assassin?"

The Spaniard smiled. "Assassin, spy, troubadour ...." he said with a bow. "A man of my profession is recognized so rarely for *all* his talents."

"You murdered Kathryn and Gaelyn!"

"Yes," Miguel hissed, "and now I am going to do what I should have done long ago."

Don Miguel threw his blade. It sped through the air, directly at Billy, catching him flat-footed. The knife stopped unexpectedly, in Billy's grip.

He stared at it momentarily, then in the blink of an eye, he flipped the weapon and flung it back to its master.

Don Miguel's smile slowly melted as he examined the knife-handle protruding from his chest. Blood ran down his shirt, then he stumbled to the side and fell over the railing into the sea. Billy recovered his wits and ran to the side, but could find no trace of the Spaniard.

At that moment, the fire flared up. Billy jumped through the flames to help Hugh. He pushed back one crate, then another, but could not find the King's Champion.

Hugh was trapped under a large crate with the fire just inches away. He tried to move the big box, but it was far too heavy. He tried to lift the crate again, but with his arms pinned he couldn't get enough leverage. He then tried to slip out from under it and found that it held him fast. Hugh craned his head to spot his opponent, and then Billy's face was peering down at him.

Billy pushed on the crate then said, "I'll get help," before disappearing into the smoke and steam.

Billy cried out to the passengers for help, but most of them cowered in the aft of the rolling ship near the captain. The only ones nearby were three desperate men struggling to get free of their tethers and escape the fire. As for the crew, they were aloft, striving to get the sails and rigging secured. Realizing that no one was coming to help, Billy sought a way to lift the heavy crate himself. He spotted a thick-handled gaff by the railing and grabbed it.

Moving as fast as he could, Billy placed the pole under one edge of the crate. The flames were still growing, and the sea seemed determined to toss the ship until it was torn asunder.

"Where's Don Miguel?" Hugh asked.

"He decided to go for a swim."

"What?"

"We were juggling knives. He missed." Billy grimly mimed the deadly blow and then set his gaff to lift the crate. "We lift on three!"

Hugh nodded and prepared to push on the crate. Then he reached for Billy's foot. "Wait!"

Billy looked at Hugh's troubled face and was reminded of the moment before he and Malcolm removed the arrow from Hugh's thigh. "*On* three!" he assured his friend.

"No, wait!" Hugh insisted.

"What's wrong?"

"You can't!"

"What?" Billy shrank from the expanding fire. "Why not?"

"Billy, don't you know?"

"Know what?"

"I am the one they sent after you. I am to bring you back!"

Billy nodded solemnly then firmly placed the gaff against the crate. "On three! One—two—"

"But I have to—"

"No buts!" Billy yelled. "We get you out of there first, then we can talk all you want! Now, one—two—three!"

Billy and Hugh pushed on the huge oak crate. It inched up, creaking as the weight began to shift off Hugh's body. Together, they forced the crate up, but it stopped moving before Hugh could free himself. Billy's gaff began to crack.

Without warning, two great hands grabbed the top of the crate. Billy looked up and saw Camion, grinning and lifting the heavy container back from Hugh. Hugh quickly rolled out from under the crate. The giant dropped the box, and it smacked the deck with a loud thump.

Camion showed Billy his crooked, toothy smile and said, "Not know little people on boat." Then as quickly as he appeared, he moved towards the bow and disappeared.

Hugh looked up at Billy. "Thank you, but you shouldn't have."

Billy shook his head and offered his hand to the King's Champion. "How could I not?" He noticed Hugh's reluctance to take his hand and opened his shirt to reveal the scars left by the dragon's claws. "Consider it a mere gesture of kindness."

Hugh took his friend's hand and stiffly got to his feet. Then staring into his face, he said, "How can treachery beget honor? Forgive me—"

At that moment, flames shot up and forced them to retreat. Hugh pointed to the three passengers who still remained tethered across the deck. "We've got to help them!"

Billy stepped forward, and the flames roared again. He looked frantically for a way to get around them, but there was none. The passengers, trapped on the other side, cried out for help.

Billy decided that, by using a tumbling trick Malcolm had taught him, he could dive over the flames. He hoped that his wet clothing and quickness would keep him from harm in the event that he slipped up.

Billy split the flames, appearing on the other side unscathed. He immediately went to the aid of the terrified passengers still tethered to the railing. *If only they had tied their ropes to the mast, the fire would have freed them by now.*

Billy went to the first passenger as Hugh ran through the flames, wrapped in a wet cloth. Billy tried to untie the rope around the man's waist, but he was hysterical and beat Billy away. Hugh grabbed the man and tried to calm him as Billy ran to the rail, but the rope was hopelessly knotted and wet here too. He examined the other two tethers and saw that they were all in the same state.

Quickly, Billy's brain sought a way to free the men. The assassin's dagger abruptly appeared in his mind, and he scanned the jostling deck. The weapon lay in some baggage near the fire, where Hugh had knocked it from Don Miguel's grip.

Billy quickly retrieved the dagger and returned. Then he hastily sawed through the first man's rope.

"He was the assassin," Billy shouted to Hugh.

Hugh released the man and gave Billy a puzzled expression. "What? Who?"

"Don Miguel killed Kathryn and Gaelyn!"

Billy cut the second and third man free. Without a word, they ran to the back of the ship and huddled with the other passengers.

Hugh's visage went from confused, to shocked, to enlightened in a single breath. Rain streamed down his face as he stared across at Billy.

"There's more," Billy said.

"What more?"

Billy took the satchel containing Sir Sedgemore's journal from his back and held it out to Hugh. "This is your father's journal."

Hugh stared at the satchel. Embossed into the weathered oilskin was the emblem of Sir Sedgemore.

Hugh reached out and took it from Billy. "Where did you get this?"

"Your father died saving the life of Queen Eleanor's child."

"The missing heir," Hugh whispered.

A wave crashed into the ship, forcing Hugh back across the deck. He quickly regained his footing and started back to Billy.

"You knew about that?" Billy said.

Hugh examined the satchel. "Until now, I only knew it as rumor."

Billy swallowed. "Hugh ... I've got to tell you. I know this will be hard for you to believe, but ..."

"What? What is it?"

Billy reached out and touched Hugh's hand. He felt the warrior's cold, wet skin, in contrast to the warmth coming from his mother's ring, and he knew Hugh's heart would accept the truth.

"Hugh, I am that missing child."

Hugh stared hard into Billy's face, through the smoke and rain. Without warning, he was looking into the eyes of his king. He had to step back to steady himself. The odd familiarity he had felt when looking upon Billy was finally illuminated, and he knew the truth.

Hugh wanted to ask a thousand questions all at once. His lips parted, but nothing came. The only thing that felt right was to bow.

At that moment, the deck between them collapsed, and Billy could see below. Steam and smoke rose out of the pit as flames licked its jagged edge.

There was a low, grinding sound that vibrated throughout the ship. Then the center mast started to lean.

Camion immediately appeared before the mast. He straddled the gaping deck and hugged the gigantic spar in an attempt to hold it in place. Hugh stared at Billy, then slung his father's journal over his shoulder and went to the giant's aid.

For a moment, their efforts were successful. However, the tossing of the ship was simply too much and the mast too heavy. With a thunderous crack, the mast broke free and fell to the aft of the ship. It threw Camion into the fiery hold and smashed the small poop deck, crushing the captain and the helpless passengers cowering there.

The collapse of the mast threw Hugh across the deck. As he scrambled to his feet, he saw Billy standing alone by the opposite railing. The aft mast creaked in sympathy with its fallen mate and shifted forward.

"Billy!" Hugh cried. "Get out of the way!" Then he frantically waved for Billy to run for the bow.

Billy glanced at the teetering aft mast and ran for the front of the ship, but it was too late. Before he could take three steps on the slippery, heaving deck, the aft mast gave way. Billy heard it over his shoulder and tried desperately to outrun it.

Hugh watched in horror as the mast slammed down on Billy's position, smiting that portion of the ship. At once, the entire hull shuddered and then exploded. Wood splinters, hot embers, water, and debris shot up into the air as the vessel broke. Hugh was catapulted from the side of the ship into the turbulent sea. As he resurfaced, he saw the remains of the *Gyldan Mene* surrender to the steadfast waves.

Hugh struggled to stay afloat. Finally he found a piece of the ship's deck floating by and dragged himself onto it.

"Billy!" Hugh shouted over the crashing sea. "Billy!"

For hours the waves pounded Hugh, making him fight just to stay atop his makeshift raft. He searched for Billy, calling his name into the darkness, but the only response came from the thunder and waves.

When Hugh had almost given up hope, he spotted something in the water. Desperately, he paddled to the object. It appeared to be a scrap of mast with a body lashed to it. As Hugh approached, he saw that it was the giant, Camion, holding the body of his captain on his chest. Camion himself was atop a portion of the deck, which was held under the water by his weight.

"Ho there!" Hugh shouted hoarsely.

Camion tilted his head up and stared at Hugh. His blackened face wore a frown as he clung to his captain's body like a child who'd been told he must give up a beloved doll.

Hugh managed to tie their rafts together. The giant said nothing and never moved again. He only stared at the sky as they drifted with the current.

By dawn, the storm had passed, and the sea was calm. Hugh was exhausted but continued to search for Billy. He found bits and pieces of the ship and the body of one passenger, but nothing more.

Midmorning, Hugh spotted land to the south and reluctantly gave up his search. After pestering, coaxing, and finally pleading with Camion, he enlisted the giant's help in maneuvering their joint craft towards the land. However, Camion insisted on "burying" his master first.

"From sea he come." The giant let the captain's body slip into the water. "To sea he goes."

It was afternoon before Hugh felt the pleasure of solid ground beneath him. He scanned the coastline, where he and Camion had landed, for any landmarks. Finding none, they decided to march eastward along the coast.

Just before nightfall, Mershore, a small fishing village on the northern shores of Lyonesse, had visitors: a morose giant and a mirthless knight.

CHAPTER THIRTY

Death of a King

Sir Hugh entered Castle Orgulous, a man unrecognizable to those who knew him. He was not the proud, splendid champion of the king who so often sallied forth from its gates. Neither was he the wrathful, hothead warrior who had recently assailed the keep in search of vengeance. Instead, he looked sullen and lowly. He still wore the dirty, torn disguise he had traded for in Dyven and rode a scruffy draft horse.

Two guards attempted to stop Hugh at the gate. He pushed back his hood and rebuked them with a no-nonsense glare. Though Hugh carried no weapons, the guardsmen fearfully backed away to let him pass.

It was much the same with everyone he met on his way to the donjon. Those who would have normally delayed Sir Hugh with some irksome question or request saw his face and suddenly remembered tasks that required their immediate presence elsewhere. This even included those who had dared to confront him on his last arrival. They scurried away before him, giving him the wide berth granted to rabid dogs. He did not appear outwardly hostile, but his most unusual appearance made them extremely wary.

Hugh rode his mount right up the steps of the main keep and dismounted. He entered the donjon and trod directly to the king's great hall. When he arrived, there were a great many nobles present. Ergyfel presided over them from the king's dais.

"We have not found your wife, Gryff," said the magister, "but we will. As for your children ..." Ergyfel stopped short when he saw the raged form of Sir Hugh emerge from the shadowy rear of the hall. "Take the prisoner to his cell," he ordered.

As Hugh continued his approach, the room became gravely quiet. All his countrymen eyed him with expressions of fear or contempt. They too parted to avoid Hugh as he marched across the floor. The king's new heir rose from the throne to greet Hugh as Gryff was dragged away by guards.

"Sir Hugh? Why, I hardly recognized you. Welcome!"

Hugh watched after Gryff. "Why have you arrested the cook? Did he burn your eggs?"

"He is a confessed traitor!"

"Where is the king?" Hugh demanded.

"Noble champion, the king is quite ill, and I—"

"I must see the king! His bloody task is finished."

Ergyfel gaped at Hugh. Slowly, his lips curled upward in a satisfied smirk. "Very well," he said, "then you shall see the king."

The King's First Counselor nodded to his right, and Hugh followed his eyes. Ergyfel's half-brother Sygeon and another man stood near the doorway. They bowed to the magister and left the hall. Hugh started across the floor to follow them.

"Sir Hugh," Ergyfel said, still beaming, "King William will be brought here."

"But you said he was ill—"

"I think he'll want everyone to hear what you have to say. After all, your quest was of concern to all the people of Lyonesse."

Hugh took a deep breath and nodded. The room began to buzz in anticipation of the king's arrival. Hugh scanned the court, looking from face to face. He wanted to know who would be present for his report—his confession. Most of the men present were minor lords, and only a few had any reputation for battle. The warrior lords of the realm were away preparing for war or already embroiled in it. The idea perturbed Hugh.

So these are to be Ergyfel's court parrots. One big, black bird, and a flock of colorful weaklings. They'll bring the kingdom to ruin. He stared at Ergyfel, his emotions churning up hate. *If only I had ...*

The king arrived, and the hall became quiet again. Six guards carried King William on a well-padded stretcher to the center of the hall. His nurse and new physician escorted him.

Hugh glared at Ergyfel. *You'll have to wait.* Then he stepped forward and knelt before the king. "Sire."

Hugh inhaled sharply when his eyes beheld the king's face. He already appeared dead. He was motionless, until Hugh spoke to him a second time, and his eyes fluttered open.

"Hugh," the king croaked softly.

"Yes, My King."

"What news? Is the battle won?"

"Battle, Sire? No, I-I have completed your quest."

"Quest ..." the king said, before he fell into a weak coughing fit.

The sight of his king tore the last shred of Hugh's hope from him. He remembered what a fine man the king had been, when he had viewed His Majesty with boyish admiration. He had been strong and fearless. *Back in the days of Queen Eleanor.*

How could such a man have killed his beloved wife? She was his entire world! Father must have been wrong. It has to be a mistake! I know King William's heart.

A tear ran down the face of the King's Champion as he gazed upon his dying master.

"Sire." Hugh girded his strength to give his report. "The boy ... Billy, is dead."

The king looked at Hugh. "What?"

"I caught up to him on a ship headed for Erin. There was a storm, and the ship went down. I and one other survived."

"And Billy?" Ergyfel asked. "How did he die?"

"He was struck by a falling mast. If that didn't kill him, then he was drowned by the sea."

The king started to cough again. "The body fails," he wheezed to Hugh, between coughs. "I'm tired."

The king leaned back into his pillow and closed his eyes. The new physician leaned forward and listened to his chest. The king's eyes snapped opened, and he swatted the doctor's head.

"I'm not dead yet, you vulture!" King William said, before resuming his position.

"Sire," Hugh said, as another tear found its way down his cheek. "I have more news. I have discovered a terrible secret, which doubly compounds my sorrow."

Hugh bowed his head, unable to look at his king. The tears began to stream from his eyes. Suddenly he felt the king's hand on his head, and he looked up.

Behind King William, on one side, stood his nurse and physician, their arms crossed, their faces scowling at Hugh. On the other side stood Ergyfel, his usual unaffected expression creased only by a thin grin and raised eyebrow.

Hugh turned his attention back to King William.

"What is it, my boy?" the king asked.

"Your Majesty, though it pains me greatly to tell you, I must. Billy—William of the Valley of the Yew—was your and Queen Eleanor's son."

Hugh collapsed on the floor as the hall erupted in shouts from the assembled lords. He lay on the cold stone floor, unable to flex a single muscle. It was as if his own words had slain him.

"My son?" King William exclaimed.

"Sir Hugh, can you confirm this?" Ergyfel shouted over the din. "Can you prove it?"

Hugh felt his father's journal resting beneath his chest. "Yes," he said, although the hall was far too loud for anyone to hear him.

The king frowned at his First Counselor then shouted in a surprisingly strong voice. "You told me he was dead, years ago!"

The lords became still. Every eye trained on the King's First Counselor.

"Well, Your Majesty—" Ergyfel said.

"You told me, your brother caught up with the kidnappers, but found my son was already dead!"

"But, Your Majesty—"

"Who the hell did we bury with my wife?"

The king fell into another coughing fit, the lords began to chatter, and, for an instant, Ergyfel appeared panicked, but then abruptly he regained his composure.

"Sir Hugh!" Ergyfel shouted. "Sir Hugh!" The lords quieted, and Ergyfel continued. "Sir Hugh, can you prove it?"

Hugh dragged himself up and pulled his father's journal from its protective case. He handed it to a nearby steward and said, "This is my father's journal. It tells how my father and Lady Enaid, under instructions from Queen Eleanor, took the baby in order to protect him. They themselves were killed, but the boy survived and was raised in the Valley of the Yew."

Ergyfel read the journal over the steward's shoulder. "This is most distressing news, Your Majesty, but I can explain."

Hugh forced himself to sit upright. "This I've got to hear."

Ergyfel glared at the King's Champion. "You see," he began, "we could not find your son, though we looked high and low."

"That is right, Your Majesty," Sygeon added. "We looked everywhere."

"So, we presumed he was dead. The child we buried was a substitute, to avoid any future *entanglements*."

Sygeon butted in again. "Impostors … civil war …"

Ergyfel frowned at his brother, then continued his explanation. "I thought it would be better, Your Majesty, *for* the kingdom. I also wanted to save you any prolonged anguish. I see now I may have been mistaken."

The king sat up and shook his fist at Ergyfel. "May have been! May have be—"

The king suddenly clutched his chest and fell back onto the stretcher. His body convulsed as he gasped for breath. Hugh and the physician sprang to his side. The physician forced a powder into King William's mouth, while Hugh clasped his hand.

"Your Majesty," Hugh pleaded. "Your Majesty!"

A moment later, the king was still. His physician listened to his chest, then smiled reassuringly to Hugh. "He will be fine now. He just needs rest."

The nurse nodded to the guards, and they lifted the king's stretcher back to their shoulders. The tiny procession left the great hall, leaving behind a quiet assembly.

Hugh wandered to the back of the great hall as the lords argued amongst themselves. He glanced back at the door through which the king had been carried. His eye caught Ergyfel, standing on the first step of the dais, surrounded by his flock, staring over their heads at the same door.

The magister's gaze slowly shifted until it fell upon Hugh. The two adversaries locked eyes, and a silent message passed between them. It read the same, both ways: *be warned!*

Hugh turned to leave the great hall. Ergyfel clapped his hands, and the lords fell silent.

"So where is the ring?"

Hugh reached for the door. The question had no meaning for him.

Ergyfel addressed him again. "Sir Hugh! Where is the ring?"

Hugh's mind was still on his dying king. "What?"

"The ring," Ergyfel said impatiently. "You were supposed to bring back the ring as proof that the boy was dead."

Hugh turned from the door. "But—"

"No!" Ergyfel shouted. "Your quest was to bring back proof of the boy's death, not excuses."

Hugh stared long and hard at his adversary. He walked towards him with slow deliberate steps. "Billy and your precious proof are at the bottom of the sea, thanks to you. What's more, I discovered that it wasn't Billy, but Don Miguel, who killed Princess Kathryn!"

All present cried out or gasped—some saying that it was hogwash, while others exclaimed their shock.

"Hush, hush!" Ergyfel signaled the nobles be still. When they were quiet, he continued. "And Don Miguel? Where is the Spaniard?"

"In Hell."

"So he is dead?"

"Yes—"

"That is all we need know. Justice is satisfied. The guilty have been punished."

The mob of Ergyfel's parrots cheered their agreement. Hugh considered the nobles and frowned. It was a waste of breath to try and tell them anything more.

Ergyfel addressed Sir Hugh in a resounding voice. "Sir Hugh, you have failed our king and our great kingdom for the last time!"

Ergyfel droned on, but Hugh was oblivious to his rhetoric. His mind was submerged in thoughts of his king, his sin against Billy, and his love, Myrredith.

"And furthermore," Ergyfel continued, "as Chancellor and sole heir, I strip you of your title as the King's Champion, and all rights, duties, and privileges accompanying that station. In addition, all lands and property now held by you are forfeit to the Crown."

"You took the land when I was a child," Hugh said, refashioning his sorrow into anger, "or have you forgotten?"

Ergyfel regarded Hugh. He perceived the muscles of the warrior's jaw growing taut. "Not broken yet," he muttered.

"Allow me to read something," said Ergyfel. He opened Sir Sedgemore's journal and read aloud: "And now, though I am surely named a *traitor*, I know I have done only what was right! I shall uphold my *vow* to the child's *mother!*"

Ergyfel closed the book. "It appears your father felt his vow to our *king* was less important than one to his *wife!* It's gratifying to see that I showed such good judgment." He turned his back to Hugh and ascended the dais. "After all, we don't want the land to fall to the son of a traitor."

Hugh's anger exploded. He grasped for his sword with one thought: to rid himself of Ergyfel once and for all. His fingers clutched at his naked side, reminding him that his sword had been lost to the sea. Suddenly, the conflagration inside him consumed all its available fuel and fizzled.

Hugh nearly collapsed. He was in shock. There had been no cries from the assembled lords—not one peep. They all stood by, quietly acceding. These men whose lives had been made comfortable, thanks to Hugh's defense of their country, were turning their backs on him. Like carrion birds, they silently watched as all his aspirations and dignity were ripped from his carcass.

"Get you hence, *Hugh.*" Ergyfel sat down on the throne. "This is a place for lords and noblemen."

Hugh turned and plodded from the great hall. He collected his shaggy mount and left the donjon. Before long, he meandered into the chapel. Hours later he was still there.

Hugh remembered coming to Orgulous, shortly after winning his spurs. He had been victorious in battle, and triumphant in numerous tournaments. In due course, he challenged and defeated the King's Champion and then took his place. It was in this same chapel that he pledged his all to serve King William.

His father had driven him all those years and, in part, all the years since. Never visible, always present, he had hung over Hugh's life like a specter. Despite what was said, Hugh could now lay his father to rest. He knew in his heart that Sir Sedgemore's honor was secure. He would haunt Hugh no longer.

Hugh had a private smile, but it didn't last long. Thoughts of what lay ahead soon brought him back to earth.

Now the kingdom was in more peril than it had ever been; the war with Gwythia was certain, King William had one foot in the grave, and Ergyfel had one cheek on the throne. Hugh knew that for the kingdom to survive, he must be more vigilant than ever. The days ahead would be grim, and the gravediggers shorthanded. Hugh prayed that King William and he would not be in need of their services.

* * *

Meanwhile, Ergyfel had entered King William's chamber with Sygeon and asked the king's doctor and nurse to wake him. When the king awoke, both Ergyfel and his half-brother knelt, waiting for King William to speak.

"What is it, Ergyfel?" the king asked weakly.

"Your Majesty, I have some rather distressing news." Ergyfel stared at the doctor and nurse until they moved to the door, out of earshot.

"Well?" the king prompted.

"I don't know how to tell you, my good Lord."

King William rolled his eyes. "Just say it!"

"Very well, Your Majesty. Sygeon has just brought me news regarding Billy."

"Does he yet live?"

"Alas no, Your Majesty." Ergyfel glanced at his brother. "But we have confirmed Hugh's report. He was indeed your and Eleanor's son."

Ergyfel held out his fist before the king. He opened his hand, revealing a small tangled cord—stained and aged grey—resting in his palm. He pulled on the ends of the cord, and all the knots were released.

At that moment, King William's mind became clear for the first time in fifteen years. His head filled with the memory of killing his beloved Eleanor with his own hands, and the sound of his voice pronouncing Billy's death sentence. They struck at him like daggers. A terrible weight descended on his heart, and he felt the icy kiss of death on his lips.

Ergyfel leaned forward and whispered to the king. "I thought you should know before you died, that it was your command and your hands that killed your son and Eleanor."

The clarity of the king's mind expanded, and he could see in great detail how Ergyfel had manipulated and destroyed him. He looked up at his cousin's gloating face and knew the horrible, damning truth. Magic or not, he had allowed Ergyfel to pull his strings, and it had cost him his beloved wife, his only son, his kingdom, and finally his life.

Ergyfel rose with a smile as the king started to slip into eternal sleep. King William watched his destroyer turn and walk triumphantly away. Hatred filled his being.

Suddenly, the king rose and grabbed a knife from the physician's tools next to his bed. His nurse gasped in astonishment, and Ergyfel looked back over his shoulder. The king was upon him, the blade of his weapon coming fast. At the last instant, the magister cringed out of the way, and his attacker plunged the knife into Sygeon's neck. Blood sprayed from the wound as both men fell to the floor.

Ergyfel's half-brother squirmed on the floor, gagging and slipping on his own ichor. Within a minute he would be dead. His slayer, the King of Lyonesse, was dead already.

"Brother," Sygeon croaked, holding out a bloody hand to Ergyfel.

Without a word, Ergyfel turned and strode from the room. He went directly to the great hall where he announced the death of King William and his own ascension to the throne.

* * *

Hugh got up to leave the chapel. He stopped abruptly at the door and knelt facing the altar.

"Lord Jesus, watch over my beloved Myrredith. And if it be your will that I should meet my death in the coming conflict, I beg you: may I gaze upon her face before I see the glory of your kingdom. Amen."

Hugh started to leave Castle Orgulous. He didn't know where he was headed, or what he would find when he got there. He just felt the need to keep moving.

A rider coming through the great gatehouse interrupted Hugh's thought. Despite his dirty, torn tunic, Hugh identified him as a royal page. Hugh could tell that the boy had been riding hard for quite some time, perhaps days. As he broke into the dim evening light Hugh recognized him as Luke, the close-lipped boy sent to fetch him after Billy's trial.

"Luke!" Hugh called.

The young page looked up, his face a mask of fear and confusion. Luke slowed his lathered mount and stopped before Hugh. He gazed about as if unfamiliar with his locale, and Hugh noticed a dark blood stain on his leggings.

"Made it," Luke said with a sigh.

Suddenly, the boy slouched and slid from the saddle. Hugh rushed forward and caught him before he could fall to the cobblestones. Gently, he laid the page on the ground and cradled him in his lap.

"Water!" Hugh yelled to a nearby servant. "And have someone fetch a doctor! Now!"

Hugh examined the boy as guards and servants crowded in around them. A servant set a bucket of water next to the boy, scooped out a bowlful, and handed it to Hugh. Hugh gingerly placed the bowl to Luke's lips and tipped it back.

Luke opened his eyes and looked up at Hugh. He turned away from the water to speak. "Sir Hugh, we are lost. The battle is lost."

"What happened? Where were you?"

"The Gwythies landed in Wyneddhamshire." Luke took a swallow of water, then continued. "The earl led us against them, but they fought like wild men—thousands of them. It was slaughter." Luke started to pass out again, and Hugh shook him.

"Where are the Gwythies headed?" Hugh asked the exhausted youth.

The boy fought to stay conscious. "They went in the direction of Dyven."

"Dyven! Myrredith ..."

Hugh grabbed the arm of a servant and pulled her down to his level. He quickly moved Luke into her lap and stood. Without a word, he mounted his horse and galloped from Castle Orgulous.

Hugh had a direction now. The last time the army of Gwythia invaded, he met them and threw them back into the sea. This time, he was determined to teach them a lesson. This time, he would show no mercy.

Without warning, an image started to expand in Hugh's mind, pushing his thoughts of blood and battle aside. All his other thoughts slid away from it like broken roof tiles, falling from a swelling tower. He spurred his mount on, his mind besieged by the image—the image of Myrredith.

Hugh left Nyraval on the King's Road, galloping in the direction of Dyven. As he crested the high pass, a strange sound penetrated his thoughts, and he stopped. Every bell in Nyraval and Orgulous rang out plaintively.

From his position, Hugh could see all of Loch Nyraval and the surrounding area. The lights of Orgulous and Nyraval glittered alone in the deepening shadows of evening. There were no armies—no threat he could detect. The bells were not an alarm. A moment of reflection and Hugh knew the meaning of the bells.

Hugh tore his ragged tunic and cried, "My King! My King." Then in a whisper added, "Godspeed."

Hugh turned his horse in the direction of Dyven and urged it forward. He never looked back.

CHAPTER THIRTY-ONE

Beyond the Horizon

Billy woke slowly, roused by the whisper of waves gently lapping on a sandy shore. He was wet and sore. He felt hard, damp wood under his face and the morning sun warming the other cheek. A memory of the *Gyldan Mene* gradually formed in his head then progressed rapidly to the storm—and Hugh—and *the fire!*

Billy sat up hastily and fell off his perch into water. He thrashed about until he realized that the water was quite shallow. The child's coffin, brought aboard the ship by Hugh, drifted next to him in the bright, clear water. Billy looked at the casket and vaguely remembered climbing on to something that had floated by in the storm.

"Sir Hugh!" Billy scanned the sparkling sea. He jumped up and ran forward. "Sir Hugh!"

The only answer was the soft lapping of waves being pushed by a cool breeze. He fell to his knees and wept.

As Billy's tears were added to the sea, his blurred vision caught them striking the water. His right hand tingled, and an image began to coalesce on the tiny ripples. Billy concentrated, and the water within the ripples became smooth as glass. Upon the surface he saw Hugh—*alive!* His noble companion looked a little worse for wear; however, he bore a very determined expression that made Billy smile. He felt a twinge from the dragon's scar on his chest and knew that someday he and Hugh would meet again.

The sound of waves again entered his consciousness, and he smelled the perfume of flowers over the briny sea. He turned and was knocked over by what he perceived. He splashed water into his face and blinked repeatedly to rid his eyes of the apparition before them.

A beach of pink sand and lavender rocks waited a few yards away. Beyond the beach stood a beautiful lush forest of giant trees. There were fat, ancient oaks between slender evergreens and varieties Billy had never seen before. Some had radiant, colorful leaves and bark that glistened like silver. Bright yellow, blue, and white flowers snuggled up against their feet like adoring children, and a multitude of eye-catching birds sang and played in their branches.

Where am I? Is this Erin? It looks more pink than emerald.

Billy dragged himself and the coffin ashore. The box was heavy and waterlogged. He considered what it might contain and shuddered. At that moment, something shifted inside, and Billy dropped it. The small coffin landed on the rocks and burst open. Sunlight flashed in Billy's eyes – reflected off silver.

Billy bent down and examined the contents that had spilled from the broken casket. There was a helmet, gauntlets, a bundle of wet clothes, and a sword. Billy eyed the sword. From the skillfully crafted bone and silver scabbard to the sparkling blue gem in the pommel, the weapon was just as breathtaking as the first time he had admired it in Sir Hugh's tent.

Billy picked up the weighty sword and pulled it half out of the scabbard. As he examined the elegant blade, a hazy memory of the first time he had held it settled on his mind. He glanced about, nervously searching the woods.

"No dragons here ... I hope." *Even so, I wish Hugh were with me.*

He turned to the sea and scanned the flat, calm waters for survivors. As far as Billy could see, there was nothing but blue sky and water.

Billy slid the sword back into its scabbard and started to put it back with the other things from the coffin. Sudden movement in the trees caught his eye, and he drew the sword. Billy watched the strange woods, his heart pounding. As he focused past the wavering tip of the heavy weapon, a fawn appeared between the trees. Billy relaxed his stance then became very still so that he wouldn't spook the young deer.

The fawn passed through the trees and headed towards the beach. Its spindly young legs wobbled as it stepped on to the loose pastel rocks. Billy held his breath.

Without hesitation, the fawn walked across the sand to Billy and nuzzled his hand. Billy was startled as the creature licked him with its rough tongue. Warily, he reached up and petted its soft, furry ears. The affectionate animal moved closer, seeming to enjoy Billy's touch.

Billy smiled at his newly found friend. A group of birds flew down from the tree line and landed on the remains of the little coffin. He continued petting the deer, but knelt to survey the birds. There were linnets, robins, sparrows, finches, and several he didn't know. They chirped at him in all their varied songs.

"Well, you're a friendly lot!"

One of the sparrows half hopped and half flew to Billy's shoulder. Billy was so surprised that he dropped Hugh's sword and fell on his rear. The excited little bird fluttered and chirped in his face before lighting once again on his shoulder. Its high-pitched twitter tickled Billy's ear.

"Welcome! Welcome!" it seemed to say.

Billy twisted his head and stared at the little bird. In turn, it cocked its head and stared back at him. Its tiny, bright eyes regarded him intelligently. Half convinced this was all a dream, Billy turned his head again and listened. The bird chirped into his ear, and once more he heard words.

"Welcome to Tirn Aill!" the sparrow piped. "Welcome, long-awaited prince!"

The bird's words were more than a greeting. They were the answer to a question—the question Billy had been asking his whole life without realizing it: *Where do I belong?*

Billy leaned back on the sand and laughed. He gazed over the quiet sea to the sun, which floated just above the horizon. It might've been the dawning of any day, anywhere in the world. Billy savored the moment and knew that it wasn't. This wasn't just any day. He wasn't just anywhere. This was his first day in Tirn Aill. He was *finally home.*

* * *

This ends Book Two.
The adventure continues with
The Prince,
Book Three of the
Jester King Fantasy Series.

I truly hope you enjoyed reading this book as much as I enjoyed writing it. If you did, I would greatly appreciate a short review on Amazon or your favorite book website. Reviews are crucial for any author, and even just a line or two can make a difference.

Thank you!

KC

ABOUT K. C. HERBEL

I write stories about adventure, magic, intrigue, danger, defeat and triumph. I also write about things that really matter, like: friends, family, love, loyalty, right and wrong, good vs. evil, patriotism, bravery, duty and honor.

†

K. C. grew up in the American Southwest and spent two decades in Southern California. He has traveled much of the U.S. and Europe (both East and West) and has worked in France, Korea, Japan, and China. Now he lives in the woods near Richmond, Virginia with his family, which includes three dogs.

ACKNOWLEDGMENTS

It has been said, that it takes a village to raise a child. I suppose the same could be said for a book, and this one is no exception. My village contains those cunning, wise, foolish and fun around me. I leave it to you to decide where you fall in, but know that without each of your contributions, this book would not be what it is.

A special thank you to Mary Anne, Stella, Leslie, and Melanie for nurturing me with love and friendship in your own unique ways. I would be negligent to not mention Shane, Jack and Robert, whose hijinks, humor and imaginations abound and have helped to lighten my mental landscape. Thanks also to Mark, Raymond and Stiles for your teaching and mentoring, and to Tom who is no longer with us. My gratitude to J.R.R. Tolkien, without whom I might not have been inspired to write Fantasy, and to C.S. Lewis whose work left a lasting impression on my heart. Lastly, to John DeChancie; thanks for your insightful advice and delightful encouragement.

K. C. Herbel
Richmond, Virginia
August 2015
God go with you!

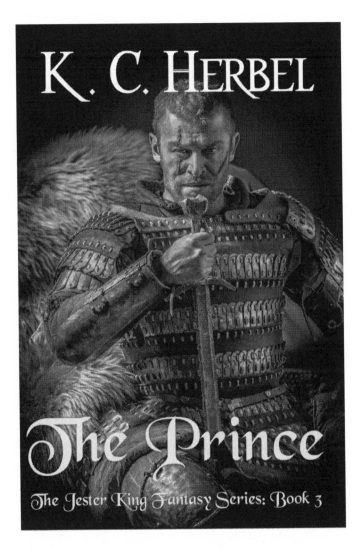

K. C. HERBEL

The Prince

The Jester King Fantasy Series: Book 3

Look for details at: www.kcherbel.com

Made in the USA
San Bernardino, CA
04 February 2018